COMES AN OUTLAW

Rie McGaha

Comes an Outlaw

Rie McGaha

Publishers Note:
This is a work of fiction. All names, characters, places, and
events are the work of the author's imagination. Any re-
semblance to real persons, places, or events is coincidental.

Copyright Marie McGaha ©2012
All rights reserved
ISBN-13: 978-0615658926
ISBN-10: 061565892X

Rie McGaha

For the outlaws I've known and loved.

Rie McGaha

~ One ~

Jake Dobbs was alive.

From the way he felt, and the number of bruises covering his body, the fact surprised him. Not to mention the amount of blood he figured he'd lost. The incident flashed through his mind—running, firing his six-shooter as fast as he could, tripping over Luke's body. His older brother lying on the cold, frozen ground, barely breathing, his shirt soaked in blood. Desperately trying to drag Luke to safety Jake was losing blood too, and simply didn't have the strength to lift his brother's dead weight. Then Luke grabbed Jake's wrist with the last bit of energy he could muster, and told him to run.

"Get out of here, Jake," Luke whispered raggedly.

"No, I'm not leaving you," Jake cried, as Luke fought the hold Jake had on his brother's bloody shirt.

"If you don't..." Luke barely managed to talk as he took a breath and choked on his own blood. "If you don't, they'll kill you too. Now go! Jake, you have to go now. Please, little brother. *For me.* Get out of here."

Jake felt his brother's body go limp. Hot tears filled his eyes and his throat burned as he choked back a sob. He left Luke on the ground and ran. He stumbled when another bullet ripped into his back near his right shoulder blade. That one almost did him in, but he was determined to live for Luke's sake.

Half running, half crawling, he finally reached dense brush and dove for cover. On his hands and knees he scrambled to the clearing where their horses were tethered, and lurched into the saddle. He tied Luke's horse to his saddle horn, and took off at a dead run. Then everything went black.

At least he recalled what happened today. Jake looked around curiously and realized he was lying on the ground in the snow, freezing his butt off. The cabin he and Luke shared stood twenty-five feet away. He could only imagine the horses knew their way home because he certainly didn't remember arriving.

Managing to roll over, he noticed the snow beneath him was almost solid red and figured the frozen ground was the only reason he hadn't bled to death... yet. Lord knew he was shivering bad enough to be frozen through. He had to get inside and take care of his wounds or he would bleed to death. Or freeze to death. Either was a good possibility right now. Jake began to crawl, or more accurately, drag himself, toward the cabin. Sweat poured down his face even as he shivered, and his bullet wounds began to bleed again.

With great deal of effort, and nearly twenty minutes of agony, he finally reached the door. Jake pulled the latch and fell inside when it opened, landing heavily on the dirty wood floor. *Well that hurt.* Not to mention the fact he'd been beaten and kicked and so his body throbbed everywhere it wasn't bleeding. Thank the Lord for the Dobbs' stubbornness.

Out of breath, he could tell his ribs were broken with every agonizing gasp, yet he somehow managed to shut the door. He leaned against the door to rest a moment and catch his breath, then made his way to the fireplace and spent fifteen long, agonizing minutes bringing the fire to life from the cold, dead ashes. He swung a kettle of water over the flames and waited tiredly for it to heat. Everything he did seemed to be in slow motion and take an overly long time to accomplish. Like struggling through quicksand. He managed to tear a clean shirt into strips for bandages and find the whiskey and a mirror. Jake was startled by his own reflection when he inspected his face. His right eye had swelled shut, his nose lay more to the left than center, and his lips were caked with so much dried blood he couldn't tell if they were cut or not. His left cheekbone had puffed up and his entire face had turned various shades of black, blue and purple. His own mother wouldn't recognize him... Nor would his brother.

Heal first, grieve later, he reminded himself.

Managing to get his shirt off, he used the mirror to examine his body. The left side of his ribcage was solid black, and the vivid purple and blue mottling on his chest and stomach were probably the result of a cowboy boot applied repeatedly. He'd been shot in the stomach, but the bullet had gone along the very edge of his skin and muscle on the left side without doing too much damage. With much grunting and swearing Jake stripped off his breeches.

He could see the bullet had gone right through his upper thigh, and it was bleeding from both the entrance and exit wounds. That left the one near his shoulder blade to contend with, and he had no idea how he was going to deal with it since he couldn't see it, and even if he could there was no way he could reach it.

Wish I had you to help right now, brother, he thought muzzily.

Rie McGaha

Gingerly, he pressed his finger to the front of his shoulder. It sent fire-like pain through the wound but at least he could feel the bullet. As he warmed up, his blood flowed more freely now, so Jake tended the other wounds before he bled to death. He could decide whether or not to dig the slug out afterward.

He pulled the cast iron pot of hot water out of the fire, dipped one of the larger pieces of cloth in it and began washing off the blood so he could see what he was fixing. Not an easy task when his vision kept getting blurry. Each movement sent a new spiral of pain through his body and he grimaced against the pain. Once the blood and dirt had been washed away, he could see his stomach just needed cleaning.

With the rapidly dirtying cloth he wiped the blood from his thigh. Once he could see the damage clearly, he pulled the cork out of a whiskey bottle with his teeth and poured the amber liquid over the wound. Gritting his teeth against a curse, he packed dry cloths around his leg and tied them in place. After taking a moment to rest and a few deep breaths, Jake doctored his stomach in the same manner.

He was so exhausted after he'd tended the wounds that he had to rest a bit again. When he pulled the blood-soaked cloths from his thigh, he could tell it wasn't going to quit bleeding on its own. He pulled his Bowie Knife from the sheath and reluctantly held it in the flames of the fire. Once the blade was red hot Jake bit down on a piece of leather and cauterized the entrance wound, screaming like a wild thing caught in a trap as the scent of burnt hair and skin filled his nostrils. He hissed through clenched teeth, then tipped the whiskey bottle to his lips and drank deeply. Almost ready for the next step, he took several gulping breaths. Heating the knife again, he then cauterized the exit wound, nearly blacking out from the pain.

Lying back weakly, he panted and tried to catch his breath. After a few minutes, Jake lifted the cloth from the wound on his stomach and saw the bleeding had stopped. He breathed a sigh of relief. Now he just needed to figure out how to care for his back.

Using his left hand he took the bottle of whiskey and poured it freely over his shoulder, letting half the liquid run down his back. Clenching his teeth tightly together, he sucked in deeply as alcohol hit raw, exposed nerves, he curled in around himself. He desperately took several calming breaths and another slug of liquid courage. What he was about to do next was going to hurt more than the other two wounds combined, and there was no way of knowing if it would even work. He did know his survival depended on stopping all the bleeding, so he had to try, or else he could bleed to death while sitting there wondering about it.

Crawling to the kitchen area, he used a stool to brace himself and struggled to a standing position. *That hurt!* The long-bladed butcher knife hung on a nail above the counter and he took it down, not really sure if he wanted to do this. Steeling himself, Jake then held the handle in his left hand and tried to reach the wound with the blade, but his ribs pulled and he couldn't manage it.

Standing unsteadily before the fireplace he carefully examined the pothook holding the kettle of water. He set the pot on the floor and pushed the rod back into the flames, then built the fire up until the hook glowed bright red. Jake lowered himself to sit with his back to it, then moved around until the end of the rod was level with the wound on his back. He pulled the pothook out of the flames, took a deep breath, and shut his eyes. Jake leaned back until the wound came into contact with the hot iron, hoping it would cauterize the bleeding. The smell of burning flesh and the intense pain took his breath, and Jake fell forward into an undignified heap on the floor just before passing out.

He awoke some time later, unaware of how much time had passed. Picking up the whiskey bottle, he took three long pulls to help with the pain, and somehow managed to get into bed. Falling into a restless sleep, Jake was just glad the bleeding had finally stopped.

The blanket was flung to the floor as he thrashed about and called out to Luke over and over again. In his fever-induced hallucinations, his mother held her arms out to him, but no matter how he tried, he couldn't reach her. The fever raged and the man suffered, walking the narrow blade between life and death as infection tortured him and his body tried to fight back. Jake relived past battles. He screamed and yelled, lashed out with his fists, fighting dream demons.

He was a child again sitting on his mother's lap... Riding his father's shoulders... Swimming with Luke in the river... They ran over fields and bloodied each other's noses... Back in the war, he stepped over bodies missing limbs and stepped over limbs missing bodies... Screaming Luke's name again, he fought through the thick, dark mist that tried to choke him and drag him under.

Rie McGaha

He fought hard, and finally, on the third day, he slept peacefully.

On the fourth day, Jake opened his eyes and looked around blearily. Time was irrelevant and he dismissed it since he had very little memory of the past several days anyway. Sitting up slowly, Jake winced from the pain in his ribs. He touched his thigh and belly to make sure they hadn't started bleeding again. The fireplace held cold ashes and he shivered as he noticed the cold. Jake held his right arm tightly against his body to cushion his aching ribs and tried not to jar himself as he made his way to the fireplace. Getting the fire started required a lot of time and energy, but the flames finally roared. He drank from the water bucket, then stumbled back to the bed, dizzy and light-headed.

Jake slept for three more days, waking for short periods of time to use the thunder mug and take sips of water. Never had he felt so weak or sick in his entire life, and he half wished he'd died in the dirt with his brother. Every time he thought of Luke new pain lanced through his heart, so much worse than the pain in his body.

Eventually he began to feel better and was able to be upright for short periods without feeling the need to puke or pass out. He managed to keep the fire going, mostly, and drank a little more water, but he was in no shape to do anything else. Though he did feel stronger as each day passed, he often felt as if it would take forever for him to heal. His patience definitely took a beating.

Nearly a month passed before he was able to hobble around and actually get outside. The fresh air had never smelled so good to Jacob Dobbs. Although

Rie McGaha

Jake found a sturdy stick to help balance himself, his thigh still hurt whenever he put weight on it. His ribs still racked with pain when he coughed or sneezed, but as long as he didn't try to take a deep breath, he was all right. Finally able to make it outside into the frozen sunshine, he ventured a little ways past the porch to peer around the cabin and see if the horses really were there, or if he'd just dreamed it. They were near a grove of trees, feeding on what grass they could find among the snow, and both were still wearing saddles and halters.

He tried to whistle for them but that hurt too much. Banging his walking stick on the ground, he tried to get their attention and hoped they didn't have saddle sores. Finally, the big bay gelding looked in his direction, and Jake continued banging the stick until the horse walked toward him, and Luke's horse followed.

When the horses reached the cabin, he rubbed the gelding's ears and leaned against him while un-cinching the saddle. Letting it slide to the ground, he unsaddled the other horse in the same way and looked them both over carefully. They didn't appear any worse for wear, and were in a lot better shape than Jake, and knowing that made him feel marginally better.

Somehow he managed to drag the saddles under the porch roof before he stumbled back inside. Though he still felt weak as a kitten, at least he recognized his own face in the mirror again. The swelling and bruising had begun to disappear and, except for the crooked nose, he almost looked normal again. Still covered in dried blood, he could smell his own stench and wanted a bath, but that would have to wait until he could stay upright for longer than a few minutes.

Hungrier than he'd ever been in his life, he grabbed more hard tack from the tin on the counter. It was getting a little tedious but there was nothing else available at the moment. Besides, his jaw hurt to chew. When he could move a little better he'd go hunting, he decided, but right now he needed to rest.

Lying on the bed he couldn't help thinking about Luke, and the pain in his heart brought tears to his eyes again. Luke was his older brother by a year, to the day, and Luke had blacked Jake's eyes for "stealing his birthday" on more than one occasion. Jake used to feel guilty for stealing Luke's birthday, but he didn't mean to steal it, and if he could've figured out a way to give it back, he would have. Jake almost smiled remembering Luke's indignant declaration it wasn't right for two brothers to have the same birthday. Since he was the oldest Luke always thought it only right he be the one that got to keep the birthday and Jake should change his.

Most of the time though, Luke took care of Jake. Watched out for him and never let the bullies pick on him. When the *War Between the States* began they joined up together and covered each other's butts. It was the reason they both managed to survive. Jake looked up to Luke, and loved him as much as a brother could. He'd not just lost his brother that night, he'd also lost his best friend.

Jake was going to kill 'em all. Every last one. He knew he would, it was just a matter of getting well and finding the men who'd murdered his brother. He knew where two of them would most likely be, and they would lead him to the others. The cockroaches probably thought he crawled off and died, but they were about to see a ghost. One very angry ghost who was going to send them all to hell. And he didn't care if it led to him swinging from the end of a rope, as long as they were all dead first.

He'd start with that fat-cat rancher, Ebenezer Franklin, the one behind Luke's death. Jake figured if he took out the man with the money the rest would fold right easy. Not that it mattered, he'd kill them all one way or the other, and there was no-where they could run or hide he wouldn't find them.

Revenge was all he thought about. Day after day as his body healed he planned, plotted and pre-pared.

Now that he was able to be up for longer pe-riods each day, he knew he'd be ready to ride by the time spring arrived. There was a little cash left, and he planned to ride south to Helena where no one knew him so he could buy supplies. He'd need am-mo, lots of it. He didn't want to purchase it any-where someone might recognize him, or have heard about what had happened to him and Luke. If he was going to be a ghost, he had to act like one.

By the time Jake was able to stay on his feet the whole day, his ribs only pulled when he coughed or sneezed. As long as he didn't make any sudden movements, he could do pretty much as he'd done before. The second day he was able to be up and about, he loaded his rifle and went to find some-thing worth eating. He came back with a couple of rabbits, which he spitted over the fire. Eating the first one whole, he saved the other for later.

Walking outside, he tried to saddle his horse. With great effort he was able to get the saddle on his gelding's back. Gasping for breath, Jake then

Rie McGaha

pulled the saddle off and stroked the animal as he used him for support. It would be a little while yet before he would be ready to ride. No matter how badly he wanted to get started hunting down the men who'd killed Luke, he knew he had to be completely healed first or all he would accomplish would be to get himself killed.

Rie McGaha

~ Two ~

Helena was muddy this time of year, and the rain came in torrents with the thunderstorms. Jake traveled the long way around the mountain to come into town from the northeast side. He hoped he wouldn't be recognized, and if he was wanted he would stay as far from Lincoln as possible. Ebenezer Franklin was a big fish in the little pond of Lincoln, Montana, and Jake didn't know if his fins reached all the way to Helena or not. He wasn't taking any chances of seeing any of the men he was gunning for until he was good and ready for them.

He took a room at the only hotel in town and paid extra for a hot bath with real soap. Though he'd scrubbed up a bit at the cabin he'd been washing in the bucket, since the creeks ran cold year round in the high country. But he'd be getting a proper bath tonight.

Opening the door for the boys who lugged the heavy tub in, he left it open while they made numerous trips with hot water. Once it was full they handed him a cake of soap and a rough towel, and left the room. Jake locked the door, peeled off his clothes, and climbed gingerly into the tub. After a few minutes he adjusted to the hot water, so he sank into it and dunked his head beneath the surface. Jake could have drowned himself right there, it felt so good. Though most of his bruises had turned horrid shades of greenish yellow by now, he still had some tender spots and he winced slightly as he used the lye soap to scrub himself clean.

Who would have thought a little hot water could feel so good? Jake thought with a little smile.

When the water became too cold for him to remain in the tub, he toweled off and dressed, then went downstairs to see about a decent meal. It had been too long since he'd eaten anything except his own cooking, he wasn't even sure his mouth would recognize real food. He'd lost a lot of weight during his recovery, probably around fifteen pounds or so from the way his clothes fit now. Well, he'd just have to work on gaining it back. And he'd get started tonight with some fried chicken, mashed potatoes, gravy, peas and biscuits followed by a couple of big slices of that hot apple pie he could smell. He ate so much he thought he'd explode, but it felt good to be full.

After a good night's sleep he left the hotel and went to the mercantile. Finding what he wanted, he purchased a Henry lever action rifle. It held sixteen rounds and he'd be able to pump the rounds out of the rifle into a man just as fast as he could lever it. He bought all the ammo the man behind the counter had for the expensive gun, and then bought all the ammo the man stocked for the pair of Smith & Wesson .44's he'd be wearing around his waist.

He'd learned to shoot when he was a young, just like all boys did. A gun was essential to survival and a man who didn't know how to use one would likely starve to death. When the war ended, he and Luke traveled west to seek their fortunes. They'd heard there was so much gold out west a man could just about walk around picking up as much as he wanted to, filling his pockets as he went. Having heard about the wild Indians, they'd been cautious but excited. They were going to be rich beyond their wildest dreams. But the stories about the gold

Rie McGaha

weren't exactly true and so the Dobbs brothers started looking for other employment.

They found it working as cowhands. The work was hard, but it did come with three hot meals a day and a bunkhouse with beds that weren't on the cold ground. They'd worked until they saved enough money between them to buy a few head of cattle of their own, which they'd taken to the high country. Having staked a claim on some good ground there, a mountainside that sloped down to a valley with a good river running through it, they built their cabin up on the mountain and let the cows run the valley. The brothers figured they were going to be rich cattle barons by the time they were through; it might have even worked if they hadn't decided to go into town that weekend.

After being up in the mountains for months they were sick of each other and wanting for female company, so they went to Lincoln. At the saloon they ordered a bottle of whiskey. Jake never really developed a taste for the stuff but Luke liked to drink it sometimes. Jake didn't gamble either, so when Luke sat in on a poker game he'd just leaned back and watched the people around him. When the sassy blonde came up to him and asked if he wanted some company, he grinned and shook his head. Money was too hard to come by as far as Jake was concerned.

What Jake liked to do when they went into town was mosey on over to Miss Mable's and sit in the library reading. Luke taunted him mercilessly about it but Jake didn't care. Miss Mable's place was comfortable and her library was quite impressive. Jake never finished school because of the war but there was no reason a man couldn't be well-read.

Rie McGaha

After the working girl went looking for another customer, Jake casually walked by the poker table, went on over to the bar and set his glass down, then slid out the twin doors and headed down the street. He hadn't gotten ten feet when he heard the first shot. He'd been wearing only a single pistol, but he had it out by the time he was back in the saloon. Luke wasn't anywhere Jake could see. Something suddenly hit him in the face and he swung, but a boot connected with his groin and brought him to the floor. Then someone proceeded to kick the shit out of him.

When he was finally alone he could taste blood in his mouth. Taking a few shallow, painful breaths, he forced himself to his feet. Holding his aching ribs he stumbled awkwardly into the street where he heard Luke shouting for him to stay back, but Jake didn't listen. He ran as quickly as he could to where Luke was trying to hide. The first bullet hit him then, going through his side and burning like a hot poker. Falling into Luke's arms he could see Luke had been shot too.

While they hid, shooting blindly into the dark, Luke explained one of the men he'd been gambling with had gotten upset when Luke won. Luke had bet everything he had since he knew he would win as he was holding four ladies, ace high. A hand like that was as good as a win, unless the man across from you held four kings, ace high. For two people to be holding hands like that with the same pot at stake, well, Luke hadn't known what the odds were but he was willing to bet the other man had cheated. And he said so.

That started a fight, and while the two men scuffled Ebenezer Franklin fired a shot to get every-

Rie McGaha

one's attention. Franklin owned everything, and everyone, in Lincoln. Everything that happened in this
town went through Ebenezer Franklin, and if it
didn't there was hell to pay. When Luke shouted
that the other man, Chet, was cheating, the other
man just sneered at him. Chet told Franklin Luke
was a liar and had lost so much money he would say
anything to keep it. There was nearly five thousand
dollars at stake. It was more money than Luke or
Jake had ever seen, much less ever had in their pos-
session.

Ebenezer Franklin told Luke to chalk it up to
experience and go on home so no one got hurt. Luke
chose to stay, and someone got hurt. The other man
was an employee of Mr. Franklin's and when Luke
killed him the firefight started. Luke figured the
odds, and ran, with all of Franklin's men in pursuit,
firing rifles and pistols both. They were the one's
who'd shot Luke. The men didn't know about Jake
until he came to find his brother.

Jake held his side to slow the bleeding and
Luke grabbed him. Even with a bullet in his shoulder
Luke wasn't hurt enough to give up. The two brothers slid down the building with their backs to it until
they were on their butts, and then scooted around
behind the other buildings, trying to work their way
back to where they could run for the thicket of brush
and cover to get back to their horses.

It was full dark now, and cold out, but that
would work in their favor. Luke told Jake to go
around the opposite side and they'd meet up where
the brush got heavy.

Jake felt the bullet rip into his thigh before
he actually heard it. He fell flat on his face in the
dirt and choked on enough of it that he couldn't

breathe for a few seconds. He lay there gasping, and hoped whoever shot him would think he was already dead.

They didn't.

Heavy footsteps ran toward him, and he could see the dusty boots of someone standing over him. Then a man grabbed Jake by his shirt and lifted him up some. Seeing he was still alive, the man dropped him and began kicking Jake in his already-bruised ribs over and over again. When Jake no longer had the strength to moan, the man hauled him up by his shirt and punched him several times in the face. Blood poured from Jake's nose and mouth until he coughed and choked. It was only when shots sounded in the distance that the man dropped Jake and took off in that direction.

Jake stayed where he was until he caught his breath and was sure no one else was around. When he figured he could manage it, he got up. Dragging his injured leg behind him while holding his ribs with one arm, Jake finally made it to where the brush got heavy. And tripped over Luke's body.

Jake shook the memory away. He had to concentrate on what he was about to do. He couldn't undo the past, only change the future. Now that he had the ammo and rifle he needed he was going back to Lincoln. The way Jake saw it, Ebenezer Franklin owed him the five thousand dollars his brother won at poker, plus Franklin's life in exchange for Luke's. And if he had to kill every man in town first, so be it. Ebenezer Franklin would die one way or the other.

Jake went back to the hotel and stopped by the kitchen to see if he could get another piece of the warm apple pie he'd had for dessert the night before. Mrs. Henderson smiled at him and went to get the pie. She lost her only son in the war and said Jake reminded her of him. He nodded and thanked her as she gave him the plate with a huge piece of pie on it.

Back in his room, he stripped down and laid the rifle on the bed next to him. The pistols were hung in their holsters on the bedpost. Propped against the headboard of the bed, with pillows behind him, Jake enjoyed the pie. He thought it would probably be a long time before he ate anything this good again.

On his way out of town he bought a bit of flour and cornmeal and tucked some coffee and sugar into his saddlebags as well. He'd need it at the cabin while he finished getting ready for his trip into Lincoln, and since he'd be home for a few days it'd be nice to have corn pone or a biscuit to go with the meat he hunted. Jake figured if he could kill a deer when he got back to the cabin, he'd roast some of it, and hang the rest so he'd have meat waiting for him when he finished his business in Lincoln. He laughed at himself. Hell, even if he didn't get killed or caught he'd still be a wanted man. There would be nowhere in Montana he could go where the law wouldn't be looking for him. Well, that was just fine with him, his chances would be better with a judge than with that shark, Ebenezer Franklin, anyway.

He rode easy back into the mountains and realized that perhaps this would be his last ride home. Strange, but he wasn't afraid of dying now. Maybe it was the fact dying wasn't just a possibility, but a foregone conclusion. He'd already lost everyone dear to him. Jake's daddy died while he and Luke

Rie McGaha

were fighting in the war. He'd been out plowing and just dropped dead, didn't even know he was sick. And it wasn't long after they'd come home from the war that their mother went to sleep one night and just didn't wake up the next morning. She was so pale and old when they came home they almost didn't recognize her. Luke said it happened that way when a husband died, sometimes, his wife just couldn't live without him and would follow him to the grave.

Jake thought about that now, and wondered if that was what happened with his parents. He wondered if a woman really could love a man so much she would die of a broken heart without him. He couldn't imagine it, and he knew he'd never get the chance to find out either. Not now. Never having loved a woman, well, at least not for more than a few hours at a time, he'd always thought one day he would. At twenty-six, he was just old enough to be thinking about a wife and family, but now, he guessed, life didn't have that in mind for him.

Late that night he finally reached the cabin and unloaded the saddlebags before unsaddling Horse. Luke had named his horse Arthur after a king in a story he was fond of, but Jake had just called his horse *Horse*. He said it was easier because Horse would never be confused about who he was. Luke thought the idea was ridiculous, but Horse didn't seem to mind.

Jake hauled everything into the cabin, but didn't bother to build a fire. It was warm enough now that he would only need a fire in the morning to heat the water to make coffee. He went to bed and fell asleep. For the first time since the shoot-out, he didn't dream of Luke lying there cold and dead in Lincoln.

~ Three ~

Julia Cavanaugh was been born and raised in Boston. She grew to be a lady who knew her place in the world. Having been raised to be a gentleman's wife she could read and write, manage a household, and host a party of any size. Perhaps she would marry a congressman, a senator, or even a president's son.

Well, that may have happened before her parents were killed in a train accident while away on one of her father's many business trips. Julia would have died with them, had she accompanied them as she usually did. Not wanting to make the trip, she'd feigned illness the day before they were to depart, so she'd been permitted to stay home in the care of her governess.

Now she lived with her father's half-brother, Uncle Ebenezer, in the most deplorable of places. Montana was definitely not civilized, and Lincoln was the dead middle of nowhere. Julia hated every minute she stayed there. But it was in Lincoln she'd remain until she either married, *fat chance she'd ever marry one of the dirty, grimy, crude, ignorant, belligerent, cowhands who worked for her uncle,* or until she turned twenty-one. Considering she needed to wait another three years before she could inherit the considerable sum willed to her by her father, it was far more likely her uncle would spend it all first.

When she moved to Lincoln to live with Uncle Ebenezer two years ago, he said he'd invested her inheritance to make even more money for them. The man had sworn to her that in time she would see just how wise he'd been, and she'd thank him for it too. Uncle Ebenezer had since become quite the

Rie McGaha

well-known businessman in Lincoln, or at least it seemed so to Julia, from the way everyone kow-towed to him when they went into town. When Un-cle Ebenezer spoke, men jumped. Julia wasn't sure what business he was in exactly, but it had appar-ently done quite well. In those two long years they'd gone from a small, two-room clapboard shack in town to the sprawling house and cattle ranch two miles out of Lincoln.

Uncle Ebenezer never discussed business in front of her, other than to tell her *the money was safe in his hands* and *she shouldn't worry*. Tutors were brought in for her, and he made sure she had the finest dresses and apparel money could buy. Not that there was a reason to wear finery anymore, the small social functions she attended in Lincoln were usually at the local church and required a minimum of finery. She'd had enough of the mundane little socials and square dances to last her a lifetime. Julia longed to be back in Boston, attending lavish balls, wearing the latest gowns from France, and dancing with fine gentleman. Being manhandled and thrown from partner to partner during a square dance was *not* her idea of fun.

Mostly, she just wanted to turn twenty-one, transfer her money into an account under her own name, and catch the first train back to Boston and the home she grew up in. She'd tried to talk her un-cle into letting her take her inheritance and move back to her house in Boston now, but he refused. Julia argued there were enough servants that she wouldn't be alone, and she'd be able to live the life she was born for.

No, Uncle Ebenezer had said, *she'd been left in his care and he wouldn't let his brother down. If she were in Boston, there'd be no one to protect her from men who would try to take advantage of a gentlewoman.*

Julia thought it was probably closer to the truth that if she were in Boston, he wouldn't have access to her money.

Feeling restless and unable to sleep, she wrapped a shawl around her shoulders and stepped out onto the veranda. The air was still, but it was cooler outside the house than in, so she walked farther out into the yard. The flowers she'd planted around the house had bloomed and their scents wafted through the air, soothing her nerves. *I am so glad I argued for my garden.* Julia sighed. Sometimes she wished something would happen just to break the monotony of her current life.

A hand covered her mouth and an arm went around her waist. She tried to scream but the noise wasn't enough to alert anyone, and as hard as she kicked, it apparently wasn't hurting whoever was kidnapping her. The arm around her waist lifted her easily off the ground and carried her through the dark, across the yard, and behind the barn.

Of course, all those dirty cowhands would be gone now, having taken the cattle up north. The only ones who could help her were Uncle Ebenezer and the old man, Buddy, who lent a hand around the ranch while his wife, Betty, cooked for the family. And she wasn't all that sure Uncle Ebenezer would help her even if he did know she needed it. After all, if she was gone the money was his to keep. It occurred to her just then that perhaps Uncle Ebenezer had done this himself, just to be rid of her.

When she was finally put on her feet again, the hand over her mouth was replaced with a bandana tied around her head. The taste of dust and sweat made Julia gag in revulsion. She felt her hands being bound in front of her and her feet tied together. Suddenly hefted like a sack of grain and thrown over a horse, Julia found she had to hold back nausea from the rough handling. The rider mounted the animal behind her and adjusted her so she was lying across his lap. *How embarrassing.* She didn't know which caused her the most mortification, the fact that she was wearing only a night rail and shawl, or the fact that her rump was bouncing up and down right there in the man's face.

The ride was interminable, though she did drift off to sleep at some point from sheer tiredness and fear.

When she woke, the sun was beginning to rise and exhaustion had set deep in her bones. Bouncing around while draped over a horse was not conducive to a good night's rest. Julia tried to look around but could raise her head only enough to see a boot stuck in a stirrup, horse hooves, and rocky ground. It certainly wouldn't help her find her way back to Lincoln when she escaped, and she would escape. The person who had kidnapped her had no idea what he was up against. If he thought she'd just stay quietly kidnapped he was so very wrong, and if this had actually been something Uncle Ebenezer planned in order to be rid of her and collect her inheritance, he would be just as sorry as her abductor.

The horse finally came to a stop and the rider slid to the ground. He hauled her down with one of his hands on her rump and took his time about removing it too. *As soon as the gag was removed from her mouth he'd definitely hear about that,* she told herself. *He may think he'd kidnapped a trollop, or maybe he was used to being with women who didn't care if he handled them so carelessly, but he was about to find out that a lady didn't put up with such treatment.*

The kidnapper sat her under a porch roof, so she was able to watch as he unsaddled his horse and stored the tack. She got her first look at him when he turned towards her, and she would have gasped if the loathsome gag hadn't been still stuffed in her mouth. His clothes might be rough and dusty but he was absolutely the most beautiful man she'd ever seen. Much taller than she would have guessed from her experience across his lap, he was also broad across the chest, and powerful, but then again she'd known that first hand. His eyes were the most intense blue she'd ever seen, and his dark chestnut hair was far too long, giving him an incredibly desirable appeal. Well, not for her, but surely some women must find that type of rugged, good looks appealing.

Still, he hadn't spoken to her at all and she had no idea who he was or why he'd kidnapped her. *It was so frustrating!* Julia's distraction led her to miss her kidnapper's approach. He hauled her up into his arms again, and he did it so easily she almost swooned. *How strong do you have to be to fling a grown woman around like a child?* Julia thought to herself as he carried her through a door.

The man put Julia on her feet next to a narrow bed, crossed to the fireplace, and began to build a fire. Looking curiously around the room, she saw two crude single beds with patchwork quilts on them, and a rough-hewn wooden table with two stools. There were no rugs on the floor and no curtains on the single window. There was a counter running along one wall that was obviously used for preparing food, while two cast iron skillets and a stew pot hung from nails on the wall. It was so bare.

After the fire roared to life, her abductor moved to stand before her with his big arms crossed over his chest. The longer he stood staring at her, the more nervous she became. Julia was beginning to think the man couldn't speak since she'd heard no sound from him since he'd kidnapped her. Trying to hold his gaze and look just as fearsome, she found those piercing blue eyes were too intense and looked nervously at the floor. *The man is too big*, she decided, which explained why her heart was pounding. He took up too much space, and therefore, too much air. Yes, that was it. That was why she felt dizzy and her heart beat at such a rapid rate. He was using up not only his share of oxygen, but hers as well.

Jake finally got his first good look at his captive and he could see just how beautiful she really was. Her long hair made him think of spun gold, and her eyes were so green they looked like something out of a child's bedtime story. In fact, he thought she looked just like a fairy tale princess. No one could've been more surprised than he to see her walk out into the yard in the middle of the night like that, and Jake admitted to himself it was a stupid impulse to kidnap her.

Luke was always saying he was reckless. He hadn't even known Ebenezer Franklin had a daughter, and when he saw her, it seemed like a sure way to get the money Jake felt he was owed. He could ransom the girl for five thousand dollars, collect the money, and then kill the man. Though he did feel sorry for the girl, he figured Franklin had enough money that she'd be well taken care of. And to Jake's way of thinking, no doubt she'd be better off without Franklin around anyway.

Continuing to stand and stare into those vibrant green eyes, his breath caught in his lungs and he couldn't have moved if he wanted to. Jake's heart began to pound. He wanted to touch her silky hair and feel every long strand slide through his fingers.

Finally, she looked at the ground and broke the spell in which those green eyes held him. He took a deep breath, cleared his throat, then slowly released the breath to give him some time to settle down and clear his head.

"I'm sorry I had to do this to you," he finally told her. "It really has nothing to do with you, but your father owes me money. When he pays the ransom I'll let you go, so don't be frightened. I'm going to take the bandana off your mouth now, please don't scream. There's no one around to hear you anyway. Do you agree?" When she nodded in agreement, he removed the gag. "Do you want some water?"

She nodded again and he held the cup to her lips. She drank greedily. "Thank you. He's not my father. He's my uncle, my father's half-brother, actually. They had different fathers you see, but he won't pay the ransom."

"You'll need to forgive me if I don't take your word for it," he said a little sarcastically.

"You *should* take my word for it because he will not pay *any* amount of ransom for me."

Jake measured her words. She sounded very certain her uncle wouldn't pay the ransom, and he didn't know what he would do with her if she were telling the truth.

"And why wouldn't he pay ransom for you?"

"Because the money is mine to begin with, and if I die, he keeps it. My uncle is a greedy man, sir, and the only reason he agreed to care for me after my parents died was the sizeable inheritance that came with me in trust. So you see, kidnapping me is of no profit to you."

Jake stared at her as her words sank in. "What's your name?"

"Miss Julia Cavanaugh. And yours?"

"Jake."

She crooked her head. "Jake what?"

"Just Jake as far as you're concerned."

Jake began to think he might have just created a bigger problem for himself than the one he already had. *Well, darn it!* Finally he decided to stick to his original plan and ransom her anyway, just to see what happened. *Not like I have anything to lose.*

Everyone in Lincoln was indebted in some way to Ebenezer Franklin and they'd do what he said, but if Jake turned the ransom demand over to the sheriff perhaps Franklin would pay rather than let the entire town know he'd rather allow his niece to die than pay a ransom for her.

"I demand you untie me, sir," Julia said in a very miffed tone of voice.

"If I do, will you promise to not try and escape?" She nodded, but he didn't believe her hoity-toity attitude. "Look, we're miles and miles from any town and there's wild animals in these mountains that will eat you as a snack. Besides, I'd just track you down and bring you back. So if you want to be untied, you'll have to tell me you promise to not run off. It's really more for your sake than mine, Julia. I'd hate for a wolf or a bear to get a hold of you." He leveled his gaze at her, hoping she'd scare.

She glared at him. "Oh, all right, I promise!"

Julia let out a disgruntled huff and attempted to stomp her foot, but since her ankles were bound she only succeeded in losing her balance and falling right into Jake's arms. Catching her easily, his hand grazed against her bare shoulder.

Grinning, he set her back on her feet and un-tied the restraints. Jake then proceeded to hobble her like he would a fractious mare. After cutting three lengths of rope a few feet long, he tied each end of one piece around one of her ankles, leaving a couple of feet of rope between her feet, then did the same to her hands, and used the last piece to tie a rope from her wrists to her ankles.

There was enough room to allow her some freedom of movement, but if she did try to run, she wouldn't get very far. He tied the loose end of the remainder of the rope from her ankle to the bed-post. She could walk to the fireplace and she could use the thunder mug, but she couldn't get close enough to the counter where knives hung on the wall.

And she's sure feisty enough to use one on me.

"This is not untying me, sir. You have hobbled me like some animal, and I demand you release me," she screeched indignant.

"Simmer down. I have to keep you here Julia, but I don't believe for a moment you wouldn't try to escape, or kill me if you could reach those knives. I have a lot of work to do and I don't want to have to worry about you." Jake made sure to sound calm and reasonable, but inside he was still smirking.

"You are *despicable*. I have never met a man so loathsome in my entire life."

"Then you've led a pretty sheltered life, haven't you?" He grinned when she turned haughtily away from him. "I have to leave now, but I'll be back. This here is rabbit stew and it doesn't taste too bad, even if I did make it myself," he said, and set the bowl and spoon on the bed beside her. "The thunder mug is under the bed when you need to use it, and I'll leave water right here for you."

When she didn't answer, he turned and shut the door behind him.

Julia looked around the cabin only after she heard the hoof beats fade into the distance. Hungry, in spite of her resolve not to accept a single thing from her captor, she picked up the bowl of stew and sniffed at it. *Smells edible...* Spooning a bit of it, she took a tentative bite. *Needs salt but other than that, tasty enough.*

When she finished eating, she set the bowl on the floor and tried not to think about her need to use the thunder mug. She would be completely humiliated when Jake returned, since he'd have to empty it for her, so she refused to use it. Walking the space between the bed and fireplace didn't take her mind off the need, and neither did bouncing on the bed. Nature's call finally won, and Julia managed to hike her gown and drop her pantaloons to use the mug.

She spent the rest of the daylight hours trying to untie the knots in the ropes. Unsuccessful at the task, she had to give Jake credit—he knew how to tie a knot. Even using her teeth she wasn't able to loosen so much as a single knot, and finally, out of frustration, gave up.

Jake had been gone all day and dark began to fall. Julia felt a little nervous being alone in the wilderness like this. What if a bear broke into the cabin and mauled her? At least at her uncle's ranch there was always somebody else around.

Wolves howled in the distance, and she swore there was something making noise right outside the cabin. Scooting back on the bed until she was in the corner, she pulled the quilt up around her until just her eyes and the top of her head showed. She hoped Jake would get back soon. She didn't like being all alone like this. Not normally so easily spooked, tonight was most certainly an exception. She was alone in a strange place and didn't like it one bit.

~ * ~

Jake waited until nightfall before venturing into Lincoln. Everything seemed to be business as usual—piano music came from the saloon and he could hear laughter and shouts from the patrons echoing down the deserted street. Leaving the safety of the dense brush, he slid silently around the back of the buildings, a gun in each hand, prepared to kill anyone who came into sight.

At the jail, he snuck up to the barred window of a cell, and listened carefully for voices inside. When he heard nothing except snoring from a prisoner, he tossed a rock with the ransom note tied around it, inside and gritted his teeth when he heard the clanging sound it made as it hit the cell bars on the other side. Jake quickly edged silently back the way he came, dove under the thicket, and ran back to Horse.

Rie McGaha

Though he rode hard all the way to the cabin, it was nearly dawn when he unsaddled Horse. Jake looked cautiously around the dark room as he entered, half-expecting Julia to be waiting to clobber him with a skillet. He put the saddle down and went to the bed just to make sure she was there. In the dim light, he could see her curled up in a tight ball, sound asleep.

After watching her a moment, he went to the other bed, tossed his clothes over the footboard, and lay down to rest.

Exhausted, he fell immediately asleep.

Sunlight filled the room and Julia squinted against the bright intrusion, then stretched and sat up on the edge of the bed. Not knowing what time it was, she thought it must be early. She hadn't heard Jake return and thought perhaps he hadn't, until she stood to use the thunder mug. She almost choked when she looked over and saw him lying there, sound asleep and bare as the day he was born.

Julia's hand flew to her mouth to stifle a startled scream. After she recovered from the shock of seeing a naked man, Julia realized she hadn't yet looked away, so she cautiously took a few restricted steps toward him for a better view. She'd never seen an unclothed man before, although she often wondered what one looked like.

Of course, she knew what happened between men and women when they were married, and her imagination was enough to drive her to distraction on more than one occasion. She often found herself day-dreaming about what it meant to be a wife and experience the physical union that would take place on the wedding night. Friends who had married sisters said it was a wife's duty and no more than that, but Candace's sister, Margaret, had said it was wonderful. Julia was intrigued and wondered if she would ever have the chance to meet a man and get married.

Now, as she stood at the foot of the bed, she was less than two feet from one and could have reached out to touch him if she wanted. Oh, she definitely did not want to—*did she? Of course not! Look away, Julia. Well-bred young ladies do not look at nude men. So why am I looking?*

His hard, male body was so different from her feminine one. He was all hard planes and chiseled muscles, with dark, crisp hair on his chest and belly. There was a scar that looked like a bullet wound on his left side, and the hair on his stomach went into a fine line below his belly button. His legs were very hairy and she noticed a nasty scar on one of his thighs.

His arms were well-defined and he had a thick neck and chiseled jaw. His cheekbones were prominent, and the stubble over his face and chin indicated he hadn't taken the time to shave in a day or two. His eyes were closed and thick lashes rested on his cheekbones. His thick hair was too long and a lock of it fell across his forehead. He was, in Julia's estimation, the most handsome man she'd ever seen.

Jake kept his eyes closed, even though he'd heard Julia move off the bed. He'd glanced at her when she first woke and she was just as beautiful in the light of day as the night before by firelight. Shutting his eyes when she stood, he heard her move toward him. He was buck naked, but if he tried to

41

cover himself now, he'd only succeed in embarrassing her, so he feigned sleep and remained where he
was. Though he managed to look at her through his
lashes, he had to fight the urge to grin when he saw
the expression on her face as she perused his body.

She studied him from one end to the other as
if he were an alien creature and he didn't know if
she approved or not, but when she sucked her bottom lip into her mouth, he almost lost control.
Somehow, he managed not to laugh, but it wasn't
easy.

He moved slightly as if he would turn over in
his sleep and Julia scurried back to her own bed.
Jake glanced over to see her lying on the bed with
her eyes closed as if she were still asleep. Grinning,
he sat up, dressed and then stood. He moved around
noisily so she would know he was no longer in bed.

When she pretended to wake up, she refused
to look at him, and he hid a grin. Her prim and proper behavior was just a façade. *This* was going to be
fun.

Rie McGaha

~ Four ~

"Good morning, Julia. Did you sleep well?" He asked, grinning at the way she blushed. Then he laughed out loud.

Irritating man! "Yes, thank you," she said primly, her chin tilted, trying to regain some composure. "Did you see my uncle?"

"No," he said, and stoked the fire, then put a rack over the flames, and placed the coffee pot on it. He filled the cooking pot with water, placed it on the iron arm and swung it into the fire next to the coffeepot.

"I'll have some water heated for you to wash up in a few moments. I have to go outside for a bit. You can use the thunder mug while I'm gone." He then turned and left the cabin.

She felt her cheeks heat at his frankness and knew her face was flaming. *How dare he speak of such things in her presence as if they were familiar with one another!*

But then again, she realized she had gazed upon his body like a wanton woman, but he didn't know that. She blushed even deeper. She was a Christian woman, went to church every Sunday and read her Bible every evening after supper. Now she bowed her head and prayed for God to forgive her for looking at the man while he slept nude. Knowing she should have simply turned away and gone back to bed until he woke, but she hadn't. Surely that was a sin she needed to repent for.

Jake was gone some time and when he returned, he carried an armful of firewood.

Rie McGaha

"Do you drink coffee? It's the only thing I have besides water. I suppose your kind drinks tea, or chocolate, or something."

"My *kind*?" She glared at him.

He grinned. "Yeah, you know. Yeah, your kind with all the high falutin' manners, and proper way of talkin'. I thought y'all drank tea and raised your little finger up in the air when you held your cup."

"Just because one is raised with manners, doesn't give you reason to mock."

"So, I offended your delicate sensibilities, did I? Well, excuse me, mi' lady, I'll try not to do it again." Then he laughed and handed her cup of coffee. "It's hot, so don't burn yourself."

"Thank you." She accepted the cup, and blew daintily on the hot liquid.

Jake noticed the perfect "O" formed by her lips, and looked quickly away.

"I can make cornmeal mush for breakfast. I've got sugar for it," he added, and pretended he was straightening up so he wouldn't have to look at her.

"Well, as wonderful as that sounds, I'll decline, thank you."

Jake heard her blow on the coffee again.

"I'll leave the hot water here on the table so you can wash. I only have a shirt and a pair of trousers that were my brother's, if you want to change. They'll be too big for you, but they're clean."

He laid the clothing on the table, and pushed the garments toward her so she could reach them. "I hate keeping you tied up like this, but I can't take the chance you'll run off and wind up hurting yourself. I'll be back in a while."

Rie McGaha

Hauling the saddle onto his shoulder, he headed toward the door, and Julia would have given anything to see the muscles bunching beneath his shirt. When he shut the door she waited until she was sure he wouldn't come back in, then pulled the nightgown up and realized he'd forgotten one very important thing. With the ropes on her wrists she had no way of taking the garment off. Sighing, she washed as best she could, then sat on the bed to wait.

Jake hurriedly dove into the icy water of the creek and came up gasping for breath. He'd dammed the stream himself to make the pool for bathing and swimming, but it ran so cold he never stayed in for long. This little dip had more to do with the girl in the cabin than the fact he needed a bath. And he hoped Ebenezer Franklin would make the deal quickly because he didn't want to spend any more time with Julia than absolutely necessary.

Even though he had great self-control, he didn't know how long he'd be able to continue exercising that control if he had to be cooped up with such a peach for much longer. She did things to his heart rate, and his blood seemed to heat whenever she looked at him with those cool, green eyes. He could see himself taking her into his arms, and kissing her senseless. Just the thought of kissing her caused him to sweat and he was still submerged in ice-cold water.

He ducked his head under the surface one more time before leaving the water, and shaking himself like a dog. After he waited a few minutes to air-dry, he dressed and slipped his feet into his boots. Then he mounted Horse and rode down the mountain.

Jake left instructions on the rock as to where he wanted the ransom dropped, and he was going to arrive very early just to make sure he wasn't double-crossed. He had the pair of .44's strapped around his waist, and the rifle lay sheathed in the scabbard on the saddle within easy reach. He tethered Horse to a tree and slipped around some giant rocks, then climbed over a log and settled down between the cleft of two boulders. He leveled the rifle toward the clearing and waited.

When he finally heard the sound of horses, he realized they'd shown up more than two hours before they were supposed to. Jake didn't recognize the first man, but the second was the sheriff. They looked around nervously. The unknown man dismounted, pulled a satchel out of his saddlebag and set it in the middle of the clearing as he was instructed. He looked nervously around, then got back on his horse and the two men rode away.

Jake sat back and waited for the better part of an hour before he moved. Picking up the rifle in one hand, he held a pistol in the other. He made his way around the clearing, checking to be sure no one was lying in wait. In the clearing, he picked up the saddlebag and then ran back into the cover of the woods, jumped onto his saddle and galloped home.

Once he had settled Horse in for the night, he opened the satchel. It was full of crumpled paper, but there was not a single dollar in sight. He pulled the paper out and threw it on the ground, cursing loudly. In the bottom of the satchel was a piece of neatly folded paper. He took it out and read—

"Release my niece and turn yourself in. I promise you a fair trial. If you do not comply by midnight, you and your brother will both die." It was signed *E. F.*

Jake sat down hard on the ground. He read the note over and over. Luke was alive. *Luke was alive? How could Luke be alive?* It had to be a joke, a trick of some kind. But if it were, how would Franklin know he was Luke's brother? He hadn't mentioned the relationship in his ransom note. Only Luke would have been able to recognize his handwriting and know it was Jake exacting his pound of flesh.

He was so overwhelmed by the revelation he didn't know what to think or do. If he didn't release Julia by midnight, Luke really would die, and if he did release Julia, Luke would probably die anyway. Unless it was a dodge and they'd somehow figured out who kidnapped Julia. Maybe they were using Luke as leverage and he really had died back there in the dirt that night.

Jake needed to think. He picked up his rifle and started walking in no particular direction. Not heading in any particular direction, he didn't know how far he'd walked, but he wasn't getting anywhere no matter how far it'd been. He didn't know if he should refuse to release Julia, and bet that it was all a trick, or take the chance that Luke was alive and do as the note said.

Walking distractedly back to the cabin, Jake went inside. He looked at Julia on the bed, sitting there looking at him so innocently, and threw the note at her without saying a word.

She flinched in reaction before she picked it up and smoothed it out so she could read it.

"You're Luke's brother?" She said looking at him.

Jake's eyes went ice cold when he looked at her, and she felt her heart stutter. She had never seen such a look of sheer hatred. Crossing the space in two strides, he grabbed her by the front of her nightgown and hauled her up against him.

"You know my brother?" He gritted through clenched teeth. Julia gulped and opened her mouth, but no words came out. He shook her. "Answer me!"

"Y-y-yes," she stammered.

He could see fear in those pretty green eyes, but he didn't release her.

"Tell me how," he demanded.

"He was shot, hurt really bad and they thought he'd die before morning because Doc had done all he could and said only the Lord could save him. I went to Doc's house every day and helped nurse him, but I didn't think he would recover either.

"His fever was so high, he was delirious and out of his head most of the time, and nothing the doc did seemed to help much. Then one of the Indians brought some kind of herb his tribe uses, and Doc wouldn't normally use Indian medicine for a white man, but Luke was so far gone, he said no matter what it did, it couldn't make him any worse. So he gave it to him and Luke started getting better the next day." She spoke so fast, she was out of breath by the time she'd finished.

Jake released her, went to the table and sat on one of the stools. He stared at her. All of the

Rie McGaha

steam had blown right out of him and he sat without speaking.

Franklin hadn't been lying. Luke really was alive.

"Where is my brother now?" He asked quietly.

"He's being held in the town jail waiting for the circuit judge to take him to trial. He was too weak to stand trial for a long time and Uncle Ebenezer wanted him strong and healthy. He said it wasn't right letting a sick man swing from a rope."

"They intend to hang him?"

She nodded. "I'm sorry. Oh, you must have gotten those scars at the same time. They told me another man was with him." She didn't realize she'd just given herself away.

Jake stood and stalked over to her. "How do you know I have scars from a bullet, or anything else?"

Her face turned a brilliant shade of red as she realized her foolish mistake. "I-I-I d-don't know."

He stood so close she couldn't move in any direction except backward as he fisted his hand in her nightgown. He was way too close and her heart pounded like a drum.

"I know exactly how you know about my scars," he said so softly, she barely heard him. But she could feel his breath against her skin. "You watched me sleeping, didn't you, Julia?"

She could feel his lips as they barely brushed her skin, sending chills down her spine. Shutting her eyes tightly, she could hardly take a breath now, but she wasn't sure if it was fear or something else. His lips continued to move over her skin, along her throat to her jaw line, and over her cheek. They

Rie McGaha

whispered over her eyelids and forehead. They moved over her nose and then they were almost, but not quite, touching her lips.

She knew she should scream, should push him away, or even kick him, but she couldn't move.

Jake released the grip on her nightgown and rested his hands lightly on her shoulders. Holding her gently, he touched his lips to hers. He heard her suck a breath, but she didn't try to stop him.

He pressed his lips to hers, and she accepted him. Then, with a deep breath, he grasped her shoulders and forced himself to break the kiss.

She looked at him with blind eyes, confused by his actions. Her lips were swollen from the kiss, and he could see she was out of breath. He lowered his forehead to hers and fought for control. It would be so easy to have her, and he *knew* she wouldn't resist him. But this wasn't some girl he'd met in a saloon, she was a lady and he had feelings for her. He wasn't sure what kind of feelings just yet, but he knew this wasn't the way to find out.

"Julia," he said on a raspy breath. "I'm sorry. I shouldn't have done that."

"Why? I-I-I..." she stammered, obviously not quite understanding what had happened.

"I have to go. I have to deal with this situation now. Look, I want to let you go, but right now I can't because you're the only leverage I have against your uncle. I'm sorry." He turned away from her, but she caught him by the sleeve.

"Jake, I've never..." she looked past him, seeming to search for words. "A man has never kissed me before. But I want you to know that no matter what happens I'm glad you were the one to kiss me first. I'll always remember you."

Her words hit him in the heart and brought him to his knees. He wrapped his arms around her again and held her, imprinting the feel of her against him. Releasing her, he pulled his knife from the sheath in his belt and cut her bonds.

When he was finished, he looked at her and said, "You're free to go."

Looking intently at him, she gently touched his face. "I'll be here when you get back."

"Julia, I don't know if I'll be back. Your uncle might kill Luke and me both."

"He said your brother drew on Vic for no reason. He said Luke was a cold-blooded killer."

"No." Jake shook his head and paced a few steps before continuing. "Vic lost the money in a card game and tried to cheat to get it back. Luke called him on it. Your uncle broke up the fight and then told Luke to get out of town. Vic drew on Luke, but he wasn't fast enough and well, I don't really have all the details because I was..."

He paused. He couldn't tell her what he'd been doing, he was sure she would laugh. "I wasn't right there with them until after Vic was dead. I ran out to find Luke and that's when I got shot the first time. I don't know who shot me, but I thought I was going to die, and I sure thought Luke had died that night."

Jake took a deep breath, and exhaled. "Julia," he said looking her in the eye. "I'm going to kill your uncle, Julia. You need to know that."

She looked away from him.

Rie McGaha

Jake picked up his saddlebags and began filling them with ammunition, then strapped on his pistols. "I've got to go," he said and opened the door.

Julia silently watched him go, but when the door shut, she jerked it open and ran outside.

"Jake!" He turned just as she launched herself into his arms and kissed him. "I'll be here when you get back."

Rie McGaha

~ Five ~

Jake rode hard down the mountain, circling as far west as he could to go south of Lincoln so he would come in on the opposite side of town. But first, he'd be visiting Franklin at home.

Leaving Horse and his brother's gelding together in a copse of pines, he knew everyone on Ebenezer Franklin's payroll would be lying in wait for him. Since Luke should still be in jail, Jake figured Franklin's men to be waiting for him in town, so the horses should be fine for now. There was a chance Luke had been moved to keep him from being rescued, but Jake would deal with that after he killed Franklin.

He slipped into the barn and looked cautiously around, but didn't find anyone waiting, so he crossed the yard to the house. When he passed the rose bushes he'd smelled when he kidnapped Julia, he hoped he would be returning to her. Trying the back door carefully, it clicked open, and he moved silently through the house. The first door he came to, he entered quietly, and then shut the door behind him.

Obviously, this was Franklin's office. *Bingo.* He went to the desk, opened the drawers, and rummaged through them. In the bottom he found an envelope with a large amount of cash, which he pocketed. At least he got back some of the cash owed Luke.

Back down the hall he found an old woman in the kitchen, and put his finger to his lips when she saw him. She looked warily at the gun in his hand, but didn't move or scream. *Thank the Lord he wouldn't have to hurt her.* He slipped out of the kitchen into the parlor and then let himself out the front door.

Back behind the barn, he mounted Horse, pulled Arthur behind him and rode to town. He didn't have a plan, or at least, the one he had didn't seem like much of a plan now. His heart pounded so hard, he thought it'd come right out of his chest.

Tethering the horses near the east end of town, he holstered both pistols so he could carry the rifle. It held sixteen shots, he could lever it quickly and didn't have to be as accurate as he did with a pistol. Anybody he shot with the Henry's was as good as dead. All he had to do was hit the sweet spot.

Not knowing where Franklin's men might be, Jake figured if Luke was still in the jail they'd be close by, waiting for him to break his brother out. Since the jail was the other side of town, this part of the plan should work. He hoped. Jake moved through the underbrush to the nearest building, the saloon where all the trouble began.

Once there, Jake slid down the west side of the saloon to find a way in. Trying a window in the back, he was surprised when it slid easily open. He left the rifle leaning against the windowpane, if everything went right, he'd be back very shortly. He crawled in as quietly as he could, pulled one pistol from its holster, and then went to the back stairs and climbed them as quietly as he could.

Some of the working girls would be downstairs still, so he checked the bedroom doors until he found one unlocked and empty. Going inside, he stood at the end of the wardrobe and waited for his prey.

It wasn't long before he heard female laughter and a man's voice as they came down the hall.
The man should be too drunk to cause any problems,
or at least he hoped so. Jake didn't want to fire a
shot if he could help it.

The door opened and from the lamplight in
the hall behind them, Jake recognized a redhead affectionately known as Ruby Red. He also recognized
the fat, bald guy who had his face in her breasts. He
was one of the men who'd been playing poker with
Luke and Vic that night.

Remaining where he was until the bedroom
door shut, Jake stifled a snort as Baldy tripped and
fell headlong onto the bed. Ruby Red laughed and lit
a lamp on the bed table. While she adjusted the
wick, Jake edged up behind her. He put a hand
around her mouth and aimed the pistol at Baldy.

"Don't say a word or I'll blow your face off,"
he sneered at the man. "Ruby, don't be scared now,
I'm not going to hurt you, darlin'. I'm going to take
my hand off your mouth, so don't make me sorry I
did, okay?" Ruby nodded and Jake released her.

"What...?"

"Just be quiet, darlin', and take this rope and
tie your boyfriend up for me." He passed her the
rope and she did as she was told. "Okay, Ruby, sit
down on the floor for a minute while I check the
ropes." She sat and Jake found she tied a good knot.
Then he gagged the man so he couldn't call out.

"Ruby, stand up."

When she did, he took her arm and twisted it
gently behind her back, holding her securely but not
hurting her. "We're going to take a walk. I just want
you to cooperate, and hopefully we can all go back
to what we were doing beforehand in just a few

minutes, okay?" Ruby nodded. "Open the door darlin' and walk down the hall to the balcony."

They went down the hall and when they
reached the little alcove near the stairwell, Jake
paused with Ruby in front of him and leaned over
the edge to see the saloon floor. There weren't too
many people inside and Jake figured most of Franklin's men were outside in the cold waiting for him.
Lucky them. But the face he was looking for sat at
one of the round poker tables sipping whiskey.

Ebenezer Franklin was right where Jake wanted him. He took Ruby and kept going. It wasn't until
they reached the bottom of the stairs that someone
noticed them.

"Boss," one of Franklin's men said uneasily.

"Stay very calm," Jake said, holding the pistol
to Ruby Red's fiery head. "Keep your hands on the
table. Both of you. Everyone else just stay right
where you are and you won't get hurt." He gently
pushed Ruby closer to Franklin.

"Hello, Jake," Ebenezer Franklin said, and
turned around very slowly. "Hiding behind a woman.
I would have figured you for a bigger man than
that."

Jake never took his eyes off the man and kept
walking Ruby slowly toward the table. Once he was
within in a few feet of his target, he said, "Okay,
Ruby, take a seat."

"And you, stand up," he told Franklin.

Franklin just looked at him coolly and refused. "Now, why should I do something stupid like
that? I don't think you'll kill me until you know for
sure your brother is alive, and if I don't show up, he
won't be for long." Franklin tossed back the rest of
the whiskey in his glass.

Rie McGaha

"You're right, I won't kill you yet," Jake
sneered, and proceeded to shoot Franklin in the
shoulder. "Now get up!"

He spun around so he could see everyone else
in the saloon. "Stay where you are and you won't
get hurt. He's the only one I'm after here. Get up
now, Franklin, or I'll shoot you again, and I'm aiming
a lot lower this time."

Ebenezer held his bleeding shoulder with his
hand and came to his feet, angrily. Jake put his hand
on the back of the man's good shoulder, with the
pistol to the back of his head.

"We're going to walk out that door and go
down to the jail and get my brother. If anyone fires
while we're walking down there, you die first. Got
it?"

The wounded man nodded reluctantly as they
walked toward the doorway. Jake held the pistol
away from them, walking sideways, looking back and
forth, while trying to see in both directions at once.
The man who had been sitting across from Ebenezer
stood to draw on him, so Jake coolly took aim and
killed him. He figured it was the man's own fault anyway.

"Ruby, darlin', you stay right where you are,"
Jake said, still watching Franklin. "If you go back upstairs and untie your boyfriend, I'll be back for you.
Understand?" She nodded with wide eyes and made
no move to leave her seat.

As they stepped out of the saloon Jake gave
Franklin his orders. "When we step out onto the
street, you tell your boys to lower their weapons or
I'm going to put another bullet in you." Jake was
shaking in his shoes, but he made sure none of it
showed. His brother's life depended on it.

When they were on the dirt street, Ebenezer held up his good hand, and called out. "Put your weapons down boys. I'm shot and he'll do it again if you fire even once. Put your weapons down!" Continuing to walk down the street, Ebenezer repeated his orders several more times before they reached the jail.

"Open the door and go in," Jake ordered him.

Ebenezer opened the door but refused to go through the entrance. Jake shook his head.

"Then you better tell them to throw down their weapons and come on out."

Ebenezer sighed resignedly and gave the order. "Put your weapons on the floor and come on out men."

Jake heard the sound of guns being dropped and three men came through the door. Jake looked at them as they eyed him. "Now, tell the rest of them to get out here," he said, and pushed Ebenezer toward the entrance. "Or you go in first. Your choice."

"The rest of you get out here and leave your guns behind." Two more men came outside, glaring at Jake.

Jake thought Ebenezer looked like he wanted to kill Jake with his bare hands and Ebenezer's face was slowly turning an ugly purple color.

Forcing Ebenezer into the building first, Jake shut the door behind them. When they were inside, Jake made Franklin draw the shades over the windows.

"Now, get me those keys on that ring over there," Jake ordered.

Ebenezer grabbed the keys and led Jake to the back where there were two cells. Only one was occupied. Luke lay on the cot, and Jake thought he didn't look good.

"Open the door." Jake pushed the older man toward the cell door. "Luke, are you all right? Luke can you hear me?" Luke turned his head and Jake saw a smile flicker across his brother's lips. "Come on big brother, we're getting out of here."

"I can't make it, Jake. They gave me something. I'm sick," Luke whispered.

Jake's temper flared. "What did you do to him, Franklin? Tell me or I'll kill you right now," he shouted and hit Franklin hard with the butt of his gun.

"It's just a little laudanum to keep him compliant." He wiped the blood from his lip with the back of his hand.

"How long have you been giving him that stuff?"

"Since the beginning. The doc gave it to him for his pain, and then he got sick when he didn't have it. It was just easier to keep giving it to him to keep him quiet."

"You coward." Jake clocked him with the gun again.

Jake had seen men after the war that had been given the alcohol and opium mixture and it hadn't been a pretty sight. They became very ill when they didn't have the concoction, or didn't have enough of it. He'd also seen the ones who tried to quit using the stuff and remembered how sick they'd become with violent nightmares, hallucinations, vomiting and diarrhea. He didn't want his brother to go through any of that.

"All right Franklin, you did this to him so you're going to help get him out of here, while I keep an eye out for your men. Come on, Luke. Let's go home."

"I can't carry him," Ebenezer protested. "You shot me, remember?"

"You should have thought of that before you held my brother hostage. Pick him up."

"What about my niece, Jake? When do I get her back?"

"When I'm sure you're not behind us. When I'm sure you aren't looking for us, I'll make sure she gets back here safely."

"And I'm supposed to take the word of a kidnapper?"

"As opposed to taking the word of a murdering rat?" Jake quipped and raised a brow.

Ebenezer didn't answer, but he did help Luke to his feet and led the way out through the back.

"We're going back to the saloon, then around behind it." Jake held a pistol in each hand now, just itching for the chance to use them.

When they passed the window he had entered the saloon through, Jake holstered one pistol, and picked up his rifle. "Keep walking due south," he instructed, staying back a few feet so he could cover their backs.

Then, thinking he saw something move, he fired. He didn't know if he'd actually seen anything or not, but he wasn't taking any chances with his brother's life, or his own.

It was full dark and difficult to see since there was no moon, but Jake had a good sense of direction and was confident they'd get there, eventually. The going was slow since Luke was too ill to walk very fast, and Franklin was getting weaker from blood loss with every step. Jake could only hope they reached the horses before either of the other men passed out. It took longer than he'd wanted, but just before dawn they reached the horses.

Jake made Franklin help him get his brother across the saddle because he was afraid Luke would never be able to stay upright and they had a long, hard ride ahead. Then he smacked Ebenezer Franklin upside the head again and sent him to the ground. He wanted to kill him so very badly, but he had his brother back, and now that Luke was alive, Jake knew he couldn't shoot an unarmed man no matter how much he needed killin'.

Jake took the reins of both horses and spurred them into a dead run. Keeping to the pace would be hard on Luke, but until he could get both of them far up into the mountains, he couldn't slow down. There may be a posse after them, and once they were back in their own territory, Jake would be able to cover up the trail so no posse could track them, but they had to get there first.

He kept Arthur as close as possible to keep an eye on Luke, and then Jake began to think about what he'd do once they were back at the cabin. Julia was waiting for him but he'd given his word he would return her safe and unharmed. Thank God he had the good sense to stop with a simple kiss. If he'd gone ahead and done what he wanted, he'd feel guilty for the rest of his life.

She would eventually meet someone and want to marry, and if he hadn't stopped when he did, it would certainly leave her very little choice as to the type of man who would marry her.

A new pain lanced through Jake's heart as he thought about returning Julia to her uncle. He wanted to keep her. He hadn't spent much time with her, but she affected him deeply. He thought any woman kidnapped would be scared to death of her captor, but Julia hadn't been afraid of him at all. She was intelligent, passionate, and the most beautiful woman he'd ever laid eyes on. If things had been different, she could've been his wife. But things weren't different and she deserved so much better than anything he'd ever be able to give her.

Backtracking and rerouting their trail on the way back to the cabin took a lot of extra time, but they arrived safely, and without leaving tracks for a posse to follow.

Julia came out of the cabin when she heard the horses, and ran to wrap her arms around Jake. Holding her for a moment, he closed his eyes and buried his face in her hair, inhaling her scent. He memorized the way she felt against him, knowing it would be the last time they would ever be so close.

Gently, he pulled away and smiled. And when she leaned in to kiss him he tried to stop her. In the end, his resolve wasn't nearly as strong as he'd thought, and he gathered her to him, wrapped his hands in her silky hair, and drank her in. When he broke the kiss, her eyes were glassy. He took a deep breath and forced himself to let her go.

"I have to help my brother."

"Oh, I'm sorry. Let me help you."

She ran around the horse to help Jake get Luke down. They each took one of Luke's arms over their shoulders, carried him inside, and laid him on the bed.

"Did you know they've been giving him laudanum?"

Rie McGaha

She looked up at him and nodded. "Yes, the doctor said it would help with his pain."

"Did he also tell you that when it's given to someone for long periods of time, they can't get by without it? That they become addicted?"

"No." She shook her head, and then touched his arm. "I didn't know that. What do we do now?"

He could see the compassion on her face and it helped to bleed the anger away. Taking a deep breath, he exhaled harshly. This wasn't her fault and he didn't know why he wanted to blame her. Maybe it would be easier to take her back to Franklin if he could convince himself he was angry with her.

"The only thing we can do is wait it out. He'll get loud and belligerent. He'll sweat, fight, and de-mand more of the stuff. He'll be sick and it'll take about four or five days before he comes to his senses again, but eventually, he will. He'll just be difficult to deal with for a while."

"I'll be here with you, Jake. I'll help you," she assured him.

Pulling off his brother's boots, Jake tried to make Luke as comfortable as possible, and to buy a little time before he told Julia he was taking her back to her uncle. He didn't know how she would react, but he hoped she didn't get hysterical and cry. He was tired. He didn't know what he wanted, or what he was going to say. *Better just to get it over with.*

"Julia, come sit with me," he said quietly, and took her hand. "I left your uncle alive. Since my brother wasn't dead, I could see no reason to kill Franklin. Since I got my brother back, I told Eben-ezer I would return you to him. So as soon as Luke is

63

well, I have to take you back down the mountain."
Why did it hurt so much to see her upset?

~ * ~

Julia sat on the edge of the bed and smoothed
the big shirt over her lap. She had been able to
bathe properly and change clothes, however big they
were, after Jake cut her bindings and left her alone.
Folding her hands primly, she straightened her spine
just as she had been taught. Her mind spun and she
didn't know what to think. She thought Jake felt
something for her, the way she did for him. But now
that he had his brother back, it seemed maybe he
wasn't interested. He knew how her uncle treated
her, that she was just a means to an end for him,
something he put up with in order to have her money. And it didn't matter to Jake, he was returning
her anyway. Julia felt a lump form in her throat, but
she refused to allow herself to cry. She would not
cry in front of Jake.

"I see," she said. "I suppose that is the best
solution to the problem after all."

Well, Jake thought, *I could handle a little
more emotion than that!* She was so controlled he
wondered how she could be the same woman who'd
been so passionate. He looked at her and saw something flicker in her eyes. Was she fighting tears? He
didn't know whether she was, but he sure was.

"I'm sorry, Julia. This is hard for me and I really wish things could be different. You deserve better than what I could give you."

"And you think that taking me back to my uncle is better?"

"I think I have to do what I know is right," he
said, folding and unfolding his hands restlessly.

Rie McGaha

"I see," she said in that same calm, detached voice. Then she stood and walked across the room. She stood with her back to him for some time, and when she turned toward him he saw fire flash in her eyes.

"Do you think I just kiss any man the way I kissed you, Jake? Did that mean so little to you? Perhaps it meant nothing at all to you. Perhaps you are so used to kissing women that I *didn't* mean a thing. But let me tell you something, Jacob Dobbs, you can take me back to my uncle, but you can't make me feel differently than I do right now. You might be the first man who ever kissed me," she declared, standing toe to toe with him, poking her finger in his chest, "you're also the first man I ever loved.

"It won't matter if you take me back, I will still love you. So you go right ahead and do the *right thing*. You go ahead and tell me what I deserve, but you're the only one for me. So next time you kiss a woman, you better be sure you're ready to keep her!"

He grasped her hand gently in his, and when she tried to break free, he simply put his arms around her and held her. She did cry then. Great, gasping sobs. He held her until she was cried out and then he gently settled her on the bed. Jake lay down beside her and held her close, cherishing the time they had left.

"I have to take you back, Julia. I'm sorry."

"I know," she whispered, and cuddled up to him. They stayed there until they eventually fell asleep.

A few hours later, Luke began yelling and they both woke. Jake leaped from the bed and went to his brother's side. Luke shook violently and sweat poured off his body. Julia dipped cloths in the pot of water and wiped his brow. Jake took a pail to the creek for cold water and brought it back to the cabin. He found Julia sprawled on her back on the floor as Luke thrashed his arms and legs.

Jake ran to her and picked her up. "Julia, are you all right?"

She caught her breath. "Yes. He just caught me off guard, it wasn't intentional."

"You stay away from him from now on, I'll tend him."

She nodded. "Are you hungry? I made some stew and biscuits while you were gone."

He looked at her with something close to surprise on his face, and nodded. "Yeah, I'm starving. What did you make stew with? There's nothing here."

She laughed. "It took a little imagination, but there were some wild onions growing down by the creek, and did you know there used to be a garden planted here?"

He nodded. "We planted a few things last year, but with my injuries, I didn't get one planted this year."

"Some of it must have volunteered. I found some potatoes growing, and a few carrots, so I used the venison. It was tough and I had to boil it most of the day, but it came out pretty good. At least you had salt." She dished up a bowl of the stew and brought it to him.

Over the next few days, they took care of Luke, sleeping when he slept and staying awake when he was delirious and calling out to no one. They fed him broth, and spooned sips of water into his mouth. They bathed him and cleaned him as if he were a baby. Within days, both were exhausted.

On the fourth day, Luke opened his eyes to find Jake sitting on the other bed with his back to the wall and a pretty blond sitting between his legs, sleeping soundly as she leaned against his chest. He grinned at the sight. The girl looked swallowed up in his shirt and breeches.

"Hey, little brother," Luke managed weakly. Jake lifted Julia over his leg onto the bed, leaped to his feet and stood beside his brother.

"Luke, how do you feel?"

"Like someone chewed me up and spit me out. I thought you were dead."

"I thought you were, too." Jake sat on the edge of the bed. "It took me a while to heal up, and I thought you were dead the whole time, or I would have been down there to get you a lot sooner."

"I'm glad you got there before they strung me up," Luke said, and then nodded toward Julia, who was now awake and sitting on the other bed with her arms wrapped around her knees. "Who's this?"

"You don't remember her?"

Luke shook his head.

"She helped the doctor by nursing you and helped keep you alive. She's the one who told me you were still alive."

"How did you meet her?"

Jake grinned sheepishly. "I kidnapped her."

Luke looked from his brother to the girl on the bed. She didn't look too upset about being kidnapped. "What do you mean you kidnapped her?"

"She's Franklin's niece and..."

"What?" Luke interrupted incredulously.

"It's a long story. She's been helping me take care of you. I'm taking her back to her uncle as soon as you're well enough to travel."

"Where are we going?"

"We can't stay here. They'll find us eventually and they'll want to hang me for kidnapping. We have to leave Montana..." Jake turned around when he heard the front door slam.

Interesting.

"She doesn't look too happy about going back to her uncle," Luke observed. Jake sighed but said nothing. Luke looked at his brother. "Hey, you and she, you haven't..."

"No." Jake shook his head. "She's going back to her uncle in the same condition I found her. It's just that I..."

"Love her?" Luke finished. Jake nodded. "And she loves you?" Jake nodded again. "Then why are you taking her back?"

"Because I gave my word I would. I went down there after you, and I shot and killed one of Franklin's men. I shot Franklin, too, and I threatened Ruby Red to get next to him. I'm pretty sure Franklin lived.

"But I gave my word that when I got you home safely, I'd take her back. It's where she belongs, Luke. She's a rich girl. She's been raised in society and she's used to having nice things I can't give her. She deserves someone who can give her everything she wants."

Luke shook his head. *I think the idiot actually means it.* "I feel like crap."

"I know. They've been doping you with laudanum for the past six months, and you know what that stuff does. You've been fighting it for four days now. I don't know if it's all out of your system yet but you look better than you have in days. Are you feeling at all hungry?"

"I could eat a little bit. I'm thirsty and my mouth tastes like something died in it. Would you get me some water?"

Jake brought a cup of water and a bowl of stew back to Luke. "If you don't mind, I'm going to go outside for a minute," Jake said.

Luke almost managed a grin as he nodded, trying to keep his head from pounding again. "Yeah, go ahead."

~ Six ~

Jake put Julia in front of him in the saddle as they rode down the mountain. She had the sulks and it was putting him on edge, even if it was nice to be able to hold her one last time. When they reached the bottom where Luke would wait for Jake, Julia waved good-bye and Horse continued his downhill trek. Jake did not want to do this. Everything in him screamed at him to stop, but he knew he couldn't. He had to return her to her uncle.

"Julia..." he began uncertainly.

"No, Jake. Don't say anything else. You aren't going to change your mind and I'm not going to change mine. You'll regret this one day," she said sadly. "I already do."

She was wrong. It wouldn't be one day—it was now. He regretted his decision but he still had to keep his word. If he didn't, her uncle would have them hunted down and killed like animals.

This way, the worst to happen would be hanging, Jake thought grimly. *Maybe her uncle would be satisfied that she was home and wouldn't pursue them any further,* Jake hoped. *At any rate, it was worth a try.* Besides, he still believed Julia would be far better off without him.

She needed a gentleman for a husband. It's what she was born and raised for. When they reached the edge of her uncle's property he reined the horse in. Jake desperately ran his hands up Julia's back and fisted them in her hair.

"I know I shouldn't do this, but I can't help it," Jake told her as he pulled her head back and kissed her. He released her slowly, and then kicked Horse in the flanks. When they were near the barn

Rie McGaha

Jake let Julia slide to the ground and reluctantly let her go. She said nothing as she stared up at him with tears streaming down her cheeks. Jake couldn't look her in the eye, couldn't look at her at all, so he turned Horse and kicked him into a gallop, leaving Julia standing there alone.

Jake and Luke had headed into the Oregon Territory where they'd heard there was plenty of game. Furs were going for a high price in Sacramento and San Francisco and they needed to more money than what Jake had stolen from Ebenezer's desk if they were going to stake out some of the land they'd heard about along the Columbia River.

First, they had to cross the Rocky Mountains and then there were at least three other ranges to cross in the Idaho country before they came to Oregon. Then they'd have to traverse the eastern desert of Oregon and more mountain ranges before they reached the Columbia River Gorge. It wasn't going to be an easy trip. They planned on trapping and hunting as they went so they would have furs to trade along the way for supplies.

As autumn came, the plan was to go as far into the Rockies as they could until the snow began to fly, then dig in for the winter to wait out the spring thaw before going farther. The brothers had figured they could reach the little settlement of Jewel, near Rattlesnake Canyon, by the time the snows caused any problems. Apparently the settlement was little more than a few shacks erected by fur traders, but they'd be able to hole up for the winter and learn more about trapping while they were there.

Jake rode silently more often than not. He thought of all that had happened since the shooting,

and he remembered Julia. It broke his heart when he
left her standing behind the barn, but he'd given his
word and if nothing else, a man had to be true to his
word or he was good for nothing. He'd certainly
made a hash of it all.

As the scenery changed unnoticed, he kept
wishing he hadn't been such an honorable man. He
wished he'd not controlled himself. And he wished
he could have made love to her real slow and sweet-
like. He still couldn't help thinking thoughts he had
no right to think. He was in love with her and no
matter how he tried to get over her, he just
couldn't.

Luke saw the look on his brother's face,
though he kept his thoughts to himself, and he didn't
know what to do. *Maybe there is nothing I can do*,
he thought as they continued their westward ride.
After putting up with Jake's moods for two more
days, Luke had finally had enough of his brother's
brooding.

"I think we should go back, Jake."

Jake looked back. "What?"

Luke pulled his horse up and leaned on the
saddle horn. "Jake, you want Julia and it was quite
obvious she wants you, so why are you actin' like a
fool and ridin' in the other direction?"

"Don't be a smart aleck, Luke. What can I
offer her? All the money we've got is what I took
from Franklin's desk, and we've got a one-room cabin in the mountains. And there's probably a warrant
out for my arrest on kidnapping charges, if not murder, too."

Rie McGaha

"Look little brother, all that might be true, but I'm telling you, if you don't go back and at least find out, it's going to tear you up for the rest of your life," Luke said and turned his horse around. *I'm not going to let Jake mess his life up this way.*
"I'm not going back, Luke," Jake called out as he watched Luke ride away. Luke didn't look back. "I'm not joking Luke. I'll go on without you," Jake threatened. Luke raised his gloved hand and waved. "Luke!" Jake turned his horse and galloped after Luke. "You're a fool," Jake said through gritted teeth as he rode alongside his brother.

Luke grinned. "I know." *Thank God that worked.*

Julia sat in her bedroom and hugged her pillow to herself. She rocked and cried, and then she got up and paced back and forth. She hadn't come out of her room since Jake delivered her to her uncle's ranch. Ebenezer had told everyone she was very distraught over the ordeal she'd been through, and she only sighed when Betty, the old cook, brought her trays of food and tried to comfort her.

All Julia wanted was to go back to the little cabin and tell Jake she loved him and she didn't even care about the money her uncle was supposed to be keeping in trust for her any longer. She wanted to tell him the only thing she cared about was him and being his wife. She would learn how to live in the mountains. It wasn't as if she was helpless, even if she did have things handed to her for most of her life. She could learn what she didn't know, and Jake could teach her what he knew. She would never be happy with any other man, and no matter what her uncle said, she would not be able to marry someone else and just forget all about what happened. The fact was, she didn't want to forget, and she didn't dare tell Uncle Ebenezer what had really happened on the mountain. She just nodded and turned to look out the window. Tears ran down her face once again as she hugged the pillow tightly to her chest and buried her face in it.

"This is crazy, Luke," Jake whispered.

"Why? You did it once, what's one more time?"

"It was an accident the first time, I didn't plan on it. This really is kidnapping. I was just trying to get even last time and she walked right into me. I *had* to take her with me," Jake explained.

"Well, just think of it as rescuing her the way you did me," Luke offered with a shrug.

"This is nuts. We really will wind up swinging from the gallows now." Jake shook his head dubiously.

"We have to go sometime little brother," Luke drawled with a grin.

"Why do I let you talk me into these things?" Jake rolled his eyes in disgust as they snuck out of the barn crouched low to the ground, crossed the yard, and stood with their backs against the house.

Luke stood look out while Jake went inside. Yeah, *he* was the one taking all the risks. Although he'd been through the house before, Jake didn't know which room belonged to Julia. He entered the house quietly and crept through the kitchen to the hallway. Jake turned the handle on the first door he came to, but it was a library so he pulled the door shut again. Hoping he wouldn't have to go through every room in the house to find her, he moved to the next door and opened it a crack. Hearing heavy snoring, he shut the door quietly.

The third door he opened was obviously Julia's, so he went noiselessly inside and shut the door behind him. Kneeling silently beside the bed he found it empty. *What the...?* Jake looked around, confused. *Where would she be at this time of night?* He stood and then walked around the room trying to find some sign of what had happened to her this time. Coming up with nothing, he shrugged, opened the window and climbed out, shutting the window behind him. He went around the corner of the house and hissed at his brother.

"She's not here," Jake whispered.

"What do you mean she's not here? Where else would she be?" The look of disbelief on Luke's face was almost funny.

"I don't know. Maybe she finally talked her uncle into sending her back to Boston," Jake guessed.

"Well, I'll be..."

"Yeah, let's get back to the cabin for now and we'll think about it later." They ran all the way to the barn, mounted their horses, and rode into the night.

The sun had begun to rise by the time they reached the cabin. The two men dismounted and unsaddled the horses, hanging the saddles on hooks under the porch roof. Jake went to the door, pulled the latch, and stepped inside. He froze and held up a hand to signal Luke. Both men pulled their weapons from the holsters on their hips, and Jake went silently to the bed where someone was obviously hiding under the blanket. Holding his pistol at the ready, Jake reached out with his other hand and quickly pulled the blanket back.

Julia started and screamed in terror when she saw the gun. Then she screamed again when she saw Jake and threw herself at him.

"Jake!" She wrapped her arms tightly around his neck and cried in relief against his shoulder.

"Julia," Jake breathed. He couldn't believe she was here in his cabin. "How did you get here? What are you doing here?"

As she continued to cry and clutch him, he kissed her cheek and smoothed his hand over her hair. Just the feel of her against him caused a lump to form in his throat.

Julia pulled away from him and looked him in the eyes. She held his face in both hands, and kissed him over and over. "You're here! How did you know?"

"Julia," Jake kissed her long and slow. "How did you get here?"

"I stole one of my uncle's horses and ran away." She said as she showered him with kisses.

"How did you know the way to get here?"

"I'm not completely inept, Jake! I did ride down the mountain with you and I memorized most of it. It did take me a little longer because I got lost once or twice," she admitted with an embarrassed little laugh. "But I finally found the way."

"Oh, Julia." He held her tightly as emotions battled for supremacy within him. Anger. Fear. Love. Dread. Relief. "That was by far the stupidest thing I have ever heard of a person doing. How could you put your life in danger like that? Don't you have a lick of sense?"

Julia looked at him incredulously as his words sank in. "Excuse me?"

"I told you once there were wild animals out here that would kill you. Did you think I told you that because I wanted to scare you? I told you that because this is dangerous land, even for someone with a weapon. A mountain lion could have pulled you right off your horse and killed you with one swipe of his paw. You are to *never* do something like that again," he ranted.

"Jake," Luke interrupted. "I think you could find another way to handle this right now, little brother."

Jake had almost forgotten Luke was there, he'd been so focused on the woman in his arms. "Yeah, you're right, Luke. I'm sorry Julia, but the thought of you being out there by yourself scared the living daylights out of me." He brought his mouth down on hers again and held her close.

"Okay then," Luke remarked with his hands shoved deep in his pockets and his eyes focused on the ceiling above him. "I'm going to go, uh, well, to do something somewhere else that's not in here." He went back outside and quietly shut the door.

"I thought you were gone," Julia said, ignoring Luke, while looking into Jake's eyes.

"I was, but I came back. I went to your uncle's ranch to kidnap you again, but you weren't there and I was afraid you'd gone back to Boston."

"You came back for me, Jake?"

He saw the surprise on her face. "Of course I came back for you, Julia. I love you and I want to marry you. If you'll have me still?"

Rie McGaha

"Oh, Jake!" She began to cry again, this time in happiness, and kissed him all over his face once again.

He brushed her hair from her cheek, cupped her face in his hands, and brought his mouth slowly down on hers. When their lips met she parted for him and his tongue delved into her mouth. She didn't know what she was supposed to do, but she remembered the way he'd looked the day she'd seen him sleeping naked on the bed, and she wanted to see him that way again.

He held Julia and ran his hands over her back, around her hips to the buttons on the front of her dress. He looked at her and smiled at the way her lips had become puffy from their kiss. Her cheeks were flushed and her eyes still moist with tears. She was so much more stunning than he remembered.

He held her gaze as he undid each button on the dress, then slid his fingers beneath the fabric and pushed the bodice over her shoulders. It slid down her body and over her hips until it pooled where she knelt. Wrapping his arms around her waist he lifted her to him until they were face to face and kissed her again as he laid her gently on the bed.

"I don't know what to do," she whispered.

"You will," he assured her.

So soft, so sweet. So beautiful. All he could think of was her. Her silky skin, her scent, and her love. He felt Julia's heart pounding against his chest while her hands moved restlessly over his back, and her nails raked against his skin.

Julia grinned happily against his chest. She might not know exactly what just happened, but she knew she had satisfied him and the thought pleased her immensely. She wanted nothing more than to always have this feeling of complete satisfaction and contentment flowing through her body. It made her feel like warm sunshine had saturated her bloodstream.

Moving so he wouldn't crush her, Jake curled his arm under her head and stroked her cheek with the other hand. "Are you all right?" The feel of Julia's body against him felt amazing. He didn't ever want to move.

"Mmm," she moaned and smiled. "I've never been better."

"I thought I might have hurt you."

"You did, but just for a moment. It was the most wonderful thing I've ever done... or had done to me," she said with a giggle.

"So you enjoyed it?"

"Very much, but I do have a question." She looked up at him as he shifted his arm and rose up on his elbow.

"What is it, sweetheart?"

"I was just wondering if this is something that is done just once in a while when two people want to have a baby, or if it's something that can be done all the time?"

He laughed, overjoyed. "It depends on the people, but generally it can be done as often as two people want to."

She was silent for several minutes and he watched her as she thought. Finally, she spoke. "How often do you want to do it?"

He grinned broadly and kissed her lovingly. "Is now soon enough?"

She nodded happily and kissed him back. "You are going to marry me now, aren't you?"

Jake nearly choked. "Yes, I will marry you."

"I was just thinking about what we did, and even though it didn't feel like sin, I know it's only supposed to be between a husband and wife. So, if we don't get married, I don't know what will happen to me."

"Nothing will happen to you, Julia." Jake held her and ran his hand over her hair. "I promise to love you forever and never let any harm come to you. So, Miss Julia Cavanaugh, will you become my wife?"

"Yes." She nodded through tears.

Luke listened cautiously at the door for a few seconds before he knocked. He wanted to make sure all was clear so he didn't intrude on a private moment between the couple. He was a little jealous, but mostly just relieved that Jake wouldn't be mooning around anymore.

Jake opened the door for him and he walked inside. They had to discuss a few things now that Jake and Julia had settled their differences. First, what were they going to do about Julia? It wasn't likely her uncle would just let the situation go unanswered again. It was also improbable that he'd believe she came willingly. So it could be assumed Ebenezer Franklin would have a warrant sworn out for not only Jake's arrest, but Luke's as well. They were deep in it, that was for sure, but at least they were in it together. Luke was confident that together they could deal with anything.

Julia suggested they all just leave and not deal with her uncle at all, but while they agreed it would solve the immediate problem, it would not solve it for long. The only thing they could do was face the situation head on, and that meant riding back to Lincoln and dealing with Franklin face-to-face. He wouldn't be expecting them, and they'd have Julia's testimony on their side as well. The circuit judge was due to make his rounds in two weeks and if they timed it right they could be in and out of Lincoln in a matter of days. The circuit judge wasn't on Franklin's payroll, so that aspect wasn't an issue. Instead, they only had to worry about staying alive until the brothers could stand trial.

The trio spent the next ten days getting ready for the trip. Julia still wanted to leave the area and not worry about anything unless they absolutely had to. Luke and Jake both tried, again and again, to explain to her that meeting the problem head on was the only way they would ever be free from her uncles' wrath. And Jake held her tightly every night and kissed away the tears that slipped down her cheeks.

Rie McGaha

~ Seven ~

They rode into Lincoln at noon.

Storekeepers came out of their shops to stand on the wooden sidewalks and watch as the trio rode by. Going straight to the sheriff's office, they told him who they were as if he hadn't a clue.

"I'm Jake Dobbs and this is my brother, Luke. I think you have a warrant out for our arrest," he said as he laid the pair of pistols he wore on the sheriff's desk. Luke did the same.

The sheriff wasn't sure what to think and sat in his chair staring stupidly up at them for a moment. "Uh, yeah," he stammered. "You boys are under arrest and I'm going to have to put you in a cell."

Jake and Luke looked at one another and then back at the sheriff. It was a ridiculous thing to say, but they guessed the sheriff was caught off guard. Jake kissed Julia then followed his brother and the sheriff to the cell.

"Julia, go home to your uncle and tell him what happened," Jake told her as she watched the sheriff lock the door. "I'll see you as soon as the judge comes 'round."

She gave him a half-hearted smile and nodded. She shut the door behind her as she left the sheriff's office and reluctantly walked out into the bright sunshine.

"Miss Julia?" She turned to see one of her uncle's men walking toward her.

"Hello, Amos." She smiled. "I was just looking to find someone to take me to my uncle's ranch. Are you going there now?"

"Yes, ma'am," he answered as his fingers clenched and unclenched the hat in his hand. "I just came into town to pick up supplies for Mister Franklin, so I have the wagon."

"Thank you. I do dislike riding without a proper ladies' saddle," she said with a smile, and he looked at the ground uncertainly.

"No, ma'am. If you'll just come with me, I'll show you to the wagon." Amos still hadn't looked directly at her.

They rode the two miles to the ranch in silence, and Amos only looked in Julia's direction when he was sure she wasn't looking at him. He thought she was the most beautiful woman he'd ever seen. If she wasn't the boss' niece, he would have thought about courting her, but the boss had been very clear the lady was not to be touched by any of the ranch hands. It didn't stop them from talking about her, or from dreaming about her, either.

She'd been gone for over two weeks and the boss said she'd been kidnapped again by Jake Dobbs, but she'd just come riding into town with both them Dobbs' boys like nothing was out of kilter at all, and it made Amos wonder what actually happened. But he wasn't about to ask Miss Julia.

They rolled up in front of the white picket fence bordering the yard in front of the sprawling ranch house. Amos helped Julia to the ground and opened the gate for her.

"Thank you, Amos," she said, gifting him with a smile he thought could outshine the sun. "I'll see myself inside." He simply nodded and watched her walk to the house.

Julia hesitated uncertainly as she put her hand on the doorknob. She straightened her shoulders, then pushed the door open and went inside. She needed to act confident, as if nothing could go wrong. Jake and Luke depended on her. The front room was dark because the draperies hadn't been pulled back. Julia crossed the room and went down the hall to her uncle's study. Taking a deep breath she knocked lightly on the door.

"Open," he called loudly, the irritation at the disruption sounding in his voice.

Julia pushed the door and walked in. "Hello, Uncle Ebenezer," she said calmly.

Ebenezer Franklin spun from his desk and stared at her in surprised shock. He looked her up and down and she could see his Adam's apple working beneath the folds of flesh covering his throat. Julia saw disappointment pass over his face and then he curved his lips into a forced smile.

"Julia, I was so worried about you!" He came toward her and hugged her. It made her flesh crawl.

She looked him dead in the eyes. "Uncle, I apologize for running away like I did, but I am in love with Jake Dobbs and I intend to marry him. He and his brother are currently in jail for kidnapping me and I know it's your doing. I want you to go to the sheriff and withdraw the charges so Jake and Luke can be released," she told him firmly.

Ebenezer Franklin walked around her to the door and pushed it shut, then turned the lock. He faced his niece and cleared his throat. "Julia, I have no intention of doing as you ask. You will not marry

Jake Dobbs because I intend to see both them
Dobbs' boys swing for interfering in my business."

Julia's mouth opened in shock. "No! You
can't. I'll take my money and leave," she cried.

"You'll take nothing." His mouth twisted into
a cruel smile. "The money is mine, girl, and I've already made arrangements for you to marry the man
of *my* choice."

Julia stiffened indignantly and glared at him.
"That money was left to me by my parents and you
have no right to it!"

Ebenezer moved faster than Julia believed a
portly man should, and he had her arm in his grasp
before she could escape. He held her so tightly she
knew there would be bruises. "You will be escorted
tonight to Helena and put on a stage to San Francisco. Once you are there you will be immediately married to Malcolm Holmes."

Julia pushed frantically against the man with
her other hand and managed to break free, sort of.
"You beast! You cannot make me marry a man I do
not know or love! I love Jake Dobbs and he is the only man I'll marry. *Let me go!*" she yelled. He already
made her give up Boston, she was *not* going to give
up Jake!

She kicked him in the shin and scratched his
face as he tried to hold her off with his free hand.
Her uncle backhanded her hard across the face and
Julia went sprawling across the floor. Ebenezer
landed on top of her and with his knee in her back
he twisted her arms behind her. Holding her wrists in
one hand, while he pulled open one of the drawers
on his desk, he pulled out a spool of packaging
twine. Ebenezer wrapped it quickly around her

85

wrists, her ankles, and left her trussed up on the
floor of the study as he moved to his desk.

He sat in his chair and pulled a handkerchief
from his pocket and mopped his face. The man was
obviously winded and his face was bright red, but
whether the color was due to anger or exertion Julia
wasn't sure. He huffed and puffed a few minutes
while trying to catch his breath.

"Julia, this could have been so much easier. If
you had just stayed gone, I wouldn't have to go to
these extremes. I need the money your parents left
you, what's left of it anyway, and the house in Boston is up for sale to cover my debts. As soon as you
arrive in San Francisco and are married to Mister
Holmes, he will wire me the ten thousand dollars he
owes me for you. Then you will go to England with
him and that will be the end of that."

Julia cried when she heard that her home was
being sold, but when she heard *she* had been sold
and being taken to England, she screamed in fury.
"You can't do that! You can't sell me like a horse or
something!" When her uncle remained unmoved she
realized it was no use and slumped despondently.
"That house is all I have left. How can you?"

Ebenezer folded a handkerchief and brutally
wrapped it around Julia's mouth to shut her up before leaving her alone in the study.

Julia fumed. She tried drumming her heels on
the floor to get Betty's attention, and when that
didn't work, on the furniture. But no one came.

her uncle returned, two of his men were with
him and they wrapped a blanket around her as if she
was a troublesome calf. Julia felt herself thrown
over one of the men's shoulder like a sack of feed

and carried outside. They loaded her carelessly in the back of the wagon, then she heard one of the men yell at the horses and the wagon lurched forward.

The wagon bounced her around mercilessly as it made its way to Helena. There, Julia was transferred to a stagecoach along with both of Ebenezer's men who were to ride with her. Her uncle bought all the seats on the coach so they would not pick up passengers along the way. Unfortunately, it reduced the chances for escape. The stage would stop only for fresh horses and the driver was to be given a bonus once they reached San Francisco.

Julia sat with her eyes closed in despair as the stagecoach bounced along. Her hands had been retied in front of her so she could sit, and her long skirts hid the ropes around her ankles. The gag on her mouth had been removed since there was no one to hear her even if she did scream. With her uncle's men sitting across from her Julia knew she had little chance of escape. She hoped she would find a way when they stopped to allow her to see to personal needs, but she really saw no way she could outrun either man, and she had no horse. The fat was certainly in the fire now. She sighed and wondered despondently how long it would be until Jake and Luke would stand trial for her kidnapping, and where she would be when both were hanged. Julia settled for gazing numbly out the window, since all her tears had long since been cried out.

Amos had been in the barn seeing to the new litter of kittens when he heard Randy and Jeff talk-

ing about taking Miss Julia all the way to San Francisco to get married.

Amos sat real still while they talked. Randy
seemed all right to him, but Jeff scared him and
Amos didn't want to be caught listening in on a private conversation. When Jeff started laughing about
how much money they'd have after making sure Miss
Julia said *I do* to the Englishman, Amos knew something was out of whack.

It was when he heard Ebenezer Franklin had
stolen all of Miss Julia's money as well as her house
in Boston, and would make sure the Dobbs' brothers
hung for kidnapping her, that Amos knew he had to
do something to help her.

Jake and Luke Dobbs had been sitting in the
Lincoln town jail for nearly two days, and it would
be another three days before the circuit judge would
be there. Neither was all that worried since Julia
would be there to testify she hadn't been kidnapped
and had left her uncle's ranch of her own accord.
However, they were getting bored and Jake wished
he'd told Julia to come back to visit him while they
waited.

Sheriff Winston brought supper in for the two
men and poured them each a cup of coffee to go
with it. "You two don't look too worried for boys
who'll be swingin' from a rope in a few days!" He
laughed, and his potbelly shook.

Jake and Luke looked at each other and then
back at Sheriff Winston. Luke asked, "What are you
talking about, Sheriff?"

"Your trial. As soon as Judge Jacobs gets here
you boys are gonna swing," the man gloated.

Rie McGaha

"Wait a minute, Sheriff," Jake said as he came up to the cell door. "Julia is going to testify she wasn't kidnapped and the judge will have no choice but to let us go."

The sheriff laughed. "Do you really think Ebenezer Franklin is gonna let y'all out of here just like that? He done sent Miss Julia off to San Francisco to get married. Ain't nobody testifying for you boys!" With that the sheriff blew out the oil lamp and walked out the front door leaving Jake and Luke in near total darkness.

"What the hell is he talking about?" Jake looked at his brother as the sheriff's words began to sink in.

Luke paced around the cramped cell space with his hands on his hips, watching his feet as he went. "I don't know, but it sounds as if we're on our own, little brother. Somehow, Franklin has managed to help himself to Julia's money and marry her off, while keeping her from testifying and sending us off to hang." Luke shook his head and laughed half-heartedly.

"Well," Jake said with a little nod, "we have two or three days to find a way to get out of here and find Julia. She's not marrying anyone but me, and I don't care what her uncle has planned. There's got to be some way out of here."

He went to the barred window, grasped the bars and tried twisting and pulling but they wouldn't budge. Even so, he only gave up once he was sweaty and panting. Jake went back to the front of the cell and shook the bars there, then kicked his tray of food across the floor petulantly.

There was no way out of the jail cell that either man could see. They sat on the bunk and talked for a while, venting their frustration at the situation, and then settled back in the silent darkness. Jake didn't sleep, but sat with his head in his hands and his eyes closed. Luke paced now and again, but eventually gave it up and lay down. Sometime late in the night they heard a sound at the window and went to see what it was. Amos Gantz stood outside trying to get their attention.

"I know Miss Julia came with you 'cause she wanted to and not 'cause you kidnapped her. This ain't right what Mister Franklin's doin' and I gotta help Miss Julia. If they find out it's me that's helpin' ya, they'll hang me instead, and they won't wait for no judge to do it. So if I help you git outta here, you gotta help me too, okay?"

Jake and Luke had no idea what the man was rambling about, but it looked like a way to get out of jail, so they agreed to help him any way they could. Amos disappeared, then, in a few minutes they heard the front door of the sheriff's office slowly open, then the little man appeared at the cell door with the keys in his hand.

"I got your horses out behind the livery," he said, turning the key and then opened the cell door. "Be real quiet. There's not many in town tonight and the sheriff's over at the saloon, so we got a chance."

Jake and Luke followed the man across the street and down the side of the mercantile to the back of the livery stable. They mounted their horses and, as hard as it was, they forced themselves to walk the animals away from town. About a hundred yards out, Jake and Luke leaned low over their saddles and spurred their horses to a full-blown run. Amos was close behind. When they finally reached the foothills and the cover of trees, they slowed to a walk and then dismounted near a stream so the horses could drink.

Luke looked at the smaller man. "Who are you?"

The man held out his hand. "I'm Amos Gantz. Pleased ta make your acquaintance." He shook their hands. "I work, er, I used to work for Franklin, but after I heard what I heard, I knew I had to help Miss Julia," he said looking at the ground. "I was sweet on her, but I knew she would never look my way. She seems to be a real nice lady."

Luke looked at Jake. Jake shrugged and stuck his hands in his pockets. "Okay," Luke said. "Why don't you tell us what it was you heard?"

Amos looked around and shrugged. "I was in the barn when I heard Randy and Jeff talkin' and they was saying how they had to get Miss Julia to San Francisco so she could marry this Englishman so he could take her off to England. Then they was going to... "

Jake grabbed the man roughly. "What do you mean *England?*"

"Jake, back off!" Luke grabbed his brother's arm and made him release the other man. "Sorry Amos, my brother's just a little bit upset." He stepped between Jake and Amos to act as a buffer. "Go ahead and tell me what else you heard."

Amos peered around Luke to make sure Jake was staying put. "I heard 'em talkin', and Franklin's real broke, and he sold Miss Julia's house that her daddy left her, and the Englishman's giving him ten thousand dollars in exchange for Miss Julia marryin' him. He's givin' ol' Jeff and Randy a bonus for gettin' her there safe and sound."

91

Rie McGaha

"I should have killed him when I had the chance. First, he gets you and me nearly killed and now he *sold* Julia? This time I am going to kill him!" Jake ranted, checking his saddlebags to make sure the ammunition he'd bought for Luke's rescue was still there.

"Jake," Luke said. "We need to get this straightened out the right way. First, we've got to find Julia before she winds up married and on a boat going to England. If you go back to Franklin's now we'll all be wanted for murder *and* kidnapping. We've got to get to San Francisco." He looked at Amos questioningly. "Well, I guess you have to make up your mind Amos. Are you going your own way or you going with us? If you go with us, I have to tell you that my brother here plans on marrying Julia himself, so if that's gonna cause a problem for you, it's best you go your own way."

Amos looked from Luke to Jake and back, and then shrugged. "Well, I would like to help Miss Julia, and if it's her own choice to marry Jake, then I guess I got no problem with that."

Jake looked up. "All right then." He held out his hand and the two men shook.

"Let's get going," Luke said and they mounted up.

Rie McGaha

~ Eight ~

Julia was hot, tired, and uncomfortable.

They'd been on the stagecoach for days and it didn't seem as if they were getting anywhere at all. Not that it would be a bad thing. The view out the window was the same as yesterday, and the day before.

She was desperately worried about Jake and Luke. Had the judge made it to Lincoln yet? She knew they'd both hang without her there to testify. She'd tried to ask her escorts if they knew anything, but they just laughed at her. *Stupid cowboys.* While they were crude, loud, and rude most of the time, at least they didn't try to touch her and they left her to herself when they stopped to stretch and take care of personal needs. She considered herself lucky in that respect, even though she still hadn't found a way to escape, at least not a way that wouldn't get her killed.

The coach continued to lurch and rock and Julia looked out the window at the dry, deserted land that seemed to stretch on forever. She could see mountains in the distance, but it had been a while since she'd seen any trees or water. She leaned her head back against the seat and closed her eyes despairingly. Suddenly, the driver yelled and the coach shot forward. Thrown across the seat, Julia desperately held on as the coach raced over rocky ground. She glanced up to see Jeff and Randy had drawn their weapons. *What the blazes was going on?*

Rie McGaha

Jeff shoved her to the floor and leaned out the window on one side, while Randy hung out the other side. They began firing as the stage rocked dangerously side to side. Julia thought bandits had attacked the coach when she heard hoof beats close to the stage. Everything became distorted as Julia hit the wall of the coach and bounced off one of the seats, only to be slammed against the floor. Something landed on her, crushing Julia to the floor. She turned to see Randy's arm beside her head. He wasn't moving and she could hardly move with his weight on top of her. *Well at least I'm not being thrown around anymore,* she thought irreverently.

"Jeff, help me," Julia gasped as she tried to wiggle out from under the other man.

Jeff didn't even spare her a glance as he continued to fire out the window. Jeff yelped and slid back inside the coach with an arrow piercing his left shoulder. He grimaced, broke the shaft and pulled the rest of the arrow out of his flesh. Only then did he notice Randy on the coach floor and lifted his head by the hair. Jeff shook his head as he peered into Randy's lifeless eyes, then pushed the body enough so Julia could get off the floor. With his knife, Jeff cut Julia's bonds and then he handed her the knife.

"If they get their hands on you they'll slaughter you—or worse. Kill yourself with the knife, it'll be easier that way," Jeff told her, then leaned out the window and continued firing.

Julia stared at the knife in her hand, her eyes wide with horror as she realized what was happening. Then the coach tilted precariously on two wheels, her hand hit the stage door, and she dropped the knife. Jeff flew out of the window when the

Rie McGaha

coach rolled over. Julia didn't know which way was up as she tumbled around inside the stage, then her head struck something hard. She felt a sharp pain, saw blinding white light, and then everything went dark and silent.

Her head pounded so badly, Julia thought it would split wide open.

Afraid to open her eyes or move, she took a deep breath and tried to mentally assess how badly she might be hurt. Aches and pains wracked her body and she wasn't sure she could move at all. She heard something in the distance but couldn't identify the sound. Lifting one hand to her head she gingerly felt her face and forehead. Not finding any serious wounds, she opened first one eye and then the other. It was dark. Julia wasn't sure where she was but she didn't see any stars above her. Turning her head she realized she wasn't in the stagecoach, but she didn't think she was lying on the ground either.

Only one way to find out, she took a deep breath, braced her hands on either side of her, and tried to scoot into a sitting position.

The effort hurt so much she may have said a curse word had her mouth not been so dry. Her head pounded so badly she thought she'd go blind. Julia kept her eyes shut until she was upright, well, nearly upright, and then slowly opened them. Her stomach lurched and her head began to spin as she took several deep breaths and fought the urge to vomit. The overwhelming desire to sleep took over. Her hand moved over what felt like soft furs as the world disappeared... and Jake came to lie beside her.

In his cabin, lying in his bed with him warm beside her, there was nothing to be afraid of when

Jake was near. She knew he wouldn't let anyone hurt her. Jake would protect her. He held her close to him and she could feel his breath on her neck. She was safe and she smiled knowing she could sleep without worry.

When she opened her eyes again, her head didn't pound the way it had earlier, but she still couldn't fight the overwhelming desire to sleep. The next time she woke, Julia had time to notice something warm covering her before she slid back into sleep again.

Julia didn't know if time had passed or not, but it didn't really matter because Jake was always there when she slept, and even though she couldn't figure out how he'd gotten out of jail, she smiled knowing he kept her safe as she slept warm in his arms.

Jake held a cup to her mouth and told her to drink. She tried, but it had such a bitter taste she almost threw up and pushed his hand away petulantly. He kept holding it to her mouth until she took a sip. It was only when she did that he let her lie down again and drift back to sleep.

Later, when he brought her a cup of water she was so thirsty she held the cup to her mouth and drank it all, even though he kept trying to take it from her.

She felt so hot and tossed the blanket away, but he covered her up again. She was burning up, couldn't he see that? Determined, she pushed the blanket away again and this time he left it off. She pulled at her dress and tried to remove it. She just wanted to cool down. Julia felt Jake's hands pull her dress off, and she lay back with a relieved sigh as he

96

put a lovely wet cloth on her face. He gave her another drink of water and she went back to sleep.

Julia tried to tell Jake her uncle had sent her to San Francisco to marry another man. She tried to tell him her uncle had sold her house in Boston. She wanted him to tell her what to do to stop her uncle from taking everything she had left. She wanted him to tell her what to do to keep from marrying the man who was supposed to take her to England and make her leave Jake behind.

But Jake didn't answer and then Uncle Ebenezer began to chase her and she tried to run but she couldn't. She screamed Jake's name over and over as her uncle grabbed her hands. She fought back. She hit him, screamed, and kicked at him. But he held her hands so tight. She fought until she wore herself out. Cool hands touched her face and a soothing voice spoke to her but she couldn't make sense of the words. Then she lost consciousness yet again.

~ * ~

Jake, Luke, and Amos rode hard for more than two days before they came to the wrecked stage-coach. Jake bailed off his horse before Horse stopped moving and scrambled up on top of the coach to look through the window, only to find it empty. He jumped back to the ground to search for Julia. Instead, he found a trunk with its lid busted open and the contents strewn around. Jake picked up some of the dresses and folded them. He didn't know if they were Julia's, but he thought they were. He tucked them into his saddlebag.

"Jake!" Luke called out urgently.

"Do you recognize him, Amos?" Jake asked when they reached the body Luke had found.

Amos nodded. "That's Jeff. Looks like he was killed when the stage rolled over him, but that there's an arrow wound in his shoulder."

"Well," Luke said as he looked around. "I'd say we should bury him, but this ground's hard as rock. We may as well just pile rocks over him to keep the animals away."

Jake helped Luke and Amos haul the rocks to the body, but he didn't like it. "He got what he deserved," Jake grumbled.

Ignoring the remark, Luke said, "Jake, see if you can find the other one. He's got to be around here somewhere."

"Sure." Jake nodded distractedly and walked toward the stage. *Where was Julia?* He picked up some more of Julia's clothing and folded them too. As he went to his horse to put them away, he noticed a boot sticking out from under the stage.

"Luke, help me! Luke, Julia might be under here too!"

The three men pushed with all their might but the stage didn't move. Amos brought his horse around, tied a rope to the coach, the other end to his saddle horn and led the horse away from the stage. The horse pulled and strained while Luke and Jake pushed and the stage began to shift. Jake's heart pounded. He didn't want to find Julia beneath it. After a few more minutes the stagecoach moved enough to uncover Randy's body, but Julia was nowhere to be found.

Thank God! Jake took a deep breath and walked away. It was great Julia had not been lying crushed under the coach, but now he had to face the fact wild Indians had probably taken her captive. It meant she was alive, but he didn't know if they'd keep her that way... and if they did, well, he'd worry about that later.

He didn't want to think the worst, but it was getting harder and harder for him to think straight with the tight fist of fear gripping his heart. He walked off into the dark, kicking rocks furiously as he went. He knew he had to get a hold of himself. Panic and fear wouldn't help Julia. In fact, they would only make it harder for him to do what needed to be done. He kicked a few more rocks, then walked back toward the stagecoach where Luke and Amos had finished burying Randy.

"Jake," Luke started.

"No, Luke, I'm okay. I know she's alive at least, and that's what matters. We'll just deal with whatever we have to deal with to find her."

"By the time we find her, she might already belong to one of their warriors."

"No!" Jake's fist lashed out at Luke's chin and then Jake landed on top of Luke. He held his brother by the shirt collar and glared at him. "I don't care! I'll kill every one of them if I have to, she's mine and..."

"It's all right, little brother," Luke said quietly. "I'm sorry. We will find her."

"Yeah," Jake nodded as he swallowed the lump in his throat. He released Luke and stood, holding out his hand to pull Luke to his feet. "Did I hurt you?"

Luke rubbed his jaw and grinned. "Not on your life."

~ * ~

Julia opened her eyes and looked around. She felt weak and tired, and there was an awful taste in her mouth. She pushed the blanket away and tried to sit up, but only made it halfway before she began to feel nauseous. She leaned on one elbow and could see she was inside, but it wasn't a house. It was... well, she wasn't sure what it was. There was a kind of door and she could see light filtering in around the edges, so she knew it was day. Hearing a noise behind her she turned her head, but moved too fast and it felt like her brain slid from one side of her skull to the other. *Well, that hurt like the dickens.* She held her head with her hand until the pain subsided, then looked at the person standing beside her.

Soft brown eyes and a kind smile greeted Julia. The girl held a cup of water for her and Julia took it thirstily. She drank it all and asked for more. The girl tried to take the cup from her but Julia refused to let it go. The girl seemed to understand and filled it with water again. Only after Julia gulped it down did she release the cup into the girl's hand. Even that little effort drained all of Julia's strength and she lay back down and shut her eyes. She'd never felt so weak, or so ill, in her whole life. *What happened?* Then memories hit her. *The stagecoach... the attack... and finally, being knocked unconscious as the coach tipped.*

Unaware of how much time had passed, Julia felt gratitude for being alive, but the overwhelming desire for sleep was still tugging at her. She rubbed her forehead to try to ease the ache, pulled the covering over her shoulders, and shut her eyes.

When she woke again it was dark, but she was thirsty and needed to use the outhouse. With some difficulty she managed to sit up and push the cover back. She rolled to her side and tried to come up on her hands and knees. Too late, she realized it wasn't a good idea. Julia began retching, though nothing came up. She felt a hand on her back and didn't care who it was at that moment. She felt so sick she thought her stomach would never stop convulsing. When she finally felt a little better, she rolled to a sitting position and then a soft light began to glow, illuminating the room. She looked around curiously and saw the same girl from earlier.

The girl motioned to her to use a bucket of some kind for her personal needs. Julia nodded, then groaned as it made her dizzy again but she had to go so badly she couldn't object. With some effort on her part, and the young girl's help with her clothing, Julia managed to relieve herself. When she finished she vaguely realized the only clothing she wore was a camisole and pantaloons, but she didn't care. She was exhausted and just wanted to sleep.

~ * ~

Jake woke early the next morning. He hadn't slept much, so when dawn began to paint its way across the eastern horizon he picked up his bedroll and tied it onto the back of his saddle. He built a small fire and spitted a rabbit he trapped over the fire to roast. The smell brought Luke and Amos awake, and after they'd shared the rabbit, the three of them searched through the wreck of the stage.

They found a few utensils, hard tack, and coffee the driver had packed under the bench. They also picked up the extra ammunition and weapons and began the search for Julia.

The ground was hard and rocky and tracks were difficult to follow. Fanning out in order to cover more ground. they hoped to find more clues to the direction the warriors had traveled with Julia. If she had been injured, and chances were she was since they'd found blood droplets on the rocks about fifty feet north of the stage, it would make traveling a little slower for her captors. Jake silently prayed they would take care of her. The blood could also mean one of the braves had been shot, but either way, the band was headed northward into the mountains. Jake also knew if they didn't find Julia before the warriors took her into the Sawtooth Mountain Range she might be lost to him forever.

He didn't know if they were looking for Shoshone, Paiute, or Ute warriors, but he hoped they weren't Crow. The Crow warriors often came into the area to raid the Shoshone camps and were vicious in their tactics. White men were afraid of the Crow, but Jake was almost sure it wasn't Crow because they hadn't found Julia's body. Crows would have raped her, murdered her, and left her body to the scavengers. He breathed a sigh of relief when that particular thought occurred to him, and hadn't even realized he'd been holding his breath.

The Sawtooth Mountains were over two miles high and heavily wooded. The three men on horseback didn't know the area, but the Indians did and could disappear into the forests without leaving a trace. Jake hoped that if Julia were injured she would slow the Indians down. If that were the case, then just maybe they'd have a chance of reaching her before the band disappeared into the mountains.

They rode until the sun began to set again but found only two more signs the Indian band had even passed that way. It was more than they'd expected. The terrain was becoming less and less desert-like and more and more mountainous. Jake never did like the desert because he felt too exposed and hopeless, but never had he hated it more than today. He

Rie McGaha

was tired but he didn't want to stop, even though it would soon be too dark to see any tracks, and that was as dangerous as lack of sleep when in unknown terrain.

He dreamed of Julia each night when he finally managed to sleep, and it took two more days, but they finally reached the forest.

Rie McGaha

~ Nine ~

Julia woke and found she was able to sit up without feeling sick, and she could see light around the door flap. The young girl smiled at her and she managed to smile back. She rolled over to her side, and got to her hands and knees. The girl helped her stand and Julia nodded with appreciation. She still felt a little dizzy and wobbled some on her feet.

When she was steady again, she looked around but didn't see her dress. She pointed to the girl's dress and then to herself. The girl smiled and retrieved a deerskin dress like the one she wore, and handed it to Julia. Julia looked at the garment and, although she didn't want to, she put it on. The girl handed her another deerskin item Julia didn't recognize until the girl pointed to her own legs, and Julia realized they were leggings to go under the dress. She needed the girl's help with them, but finally got them on. Then she slipped on the moccasins the girl provided.

Julia smiled. Although she still didn't feel like her old self, she needed some fresh air and pointed to the door. The girl nodded and pulled the flap open, then followed Julia outside. Looking around, Julia found herself to be in the middle of an Indian village, and her eyes went wide. Her first thought was that there were no teepees, and she almost laughed at herself. She looked at the room she had been in and saw that it was a wooden framed hut covered with animal skins, and all of the others seemed very similar.

The young girl took Julia by the hand and led her to another much larger hut, so she followed the girl inside. Julia realized it was the Indian equivalent of a kitchen and dining hall. The girl showed Julia where to sit and brought a carved wooden bowl filled with stew. Julia accepted it and the crude wooden spoon and dubiously took a bite. She was surprised to find it was good, but even so, she could only eat a few bites. She'd been too sick for too long to handle eating a full portion yet.

The girl looked confused when Julia pushed the bowl away.

Julia tapped her stomach and made a face. "I still feel sick."

The girl seemed to understand and said something in her own language that Julia didn't understand. The girl nodded and smiled, then took Julia by the hand and led her back to the hut. The girl pointed to the hut and said something in her own language, then repeated it until Julia repeated it back to her. The girl smiled, opened the flap and Julia went inside. She sat down on the pile of furs and removed the leather clothing the girl had given her and laid down. She was tired from the little bit of walking, and felt as if she'd just hiked miles over a mountain. Exhausted, Julia closed her eyes and went back to sleep.

Over the next several days Julia was able to stay up for longer periods of time, and the young girl, whose name was Calling Bird, continued to teach Julia the Indian tribe's language. Quick to catch on to the names of things such as trees, rocks, water and deer, Julia found that putting sentences together proved much more difficult. By the end of her first week out of bed, Julia was nearly feeling like her old self again, and helped with the cooking and cleaning, as well as caring for the younger children.

Julia enjoyed taking care of the children and discovered that once a child was weaned from the breast, all of the females of the tribe became responsible for his or her care. Julia learned games from the older children and taught the energetic youngsters games she knew as well. She also taught them her language and drew pictures for them on the ground. She was treated well by all the people of the tribe and, except for wishing she could be with Jake, she found it much more pleasurable to be with the Indians than with her uncle.

Julia learned to tan hides, clean rabbits, squirrels and birds, and to prepare them for meals. Free to come and go at will, she took walks in the forest and often went with the older children to pick wild berries or swim in the river. By the end of the second week with the Indians, Julia had learned more of the language. Though she still had trouble making herself understood to the other women, the children always seemed to know what she meant. Calling Bird also seemed to understand and continued to help Julia, who was now called *White Dove*. Julia thought White Dove was a beautiful name and didn't really mind the change.

By the end of the third week Julia began to feel sick again. She worried until she realized she'd not had her monthly courses since before she'd run away from her uncle's house and gone back to the cabin to be with Jake. She put a hand on her stomach and smiled. She was having Jake's baby! She was thrilled even though she was throwing up regularly every morning. It soothed her to know she would always have a part of Jake with her. Calling Bird un-

Rie McGaha

derstood immediately and went to tell the old woman, Winter Flower, who then told the leader of the tribe, Runs Like Wind. He called Calling Bird and White Dove to him and announced that White Dove would marry Hunts In Sky immediately.

White Dove earnestly tried to make them understand that she did not want to marry anyone except Jake but no one seemed to understand, or they just ignored her altogether. By the end of the fourth week White Dove and Hunts In Sky were married by Runs Like Wind without Julia saying a single word. She stood in the wedding lodge and waited on Hunts In Sky. She knew what was expected of her and didn't plan on fighting him, but when he came to her, he sat across from her and didn't try to touch her.

Confused, Julia accepted that he wasn't going to try to make love to her with a sigh of relief. The next day she asked Calling Bird and found that Hunts In Sky had no desire to be married to her either as he was in love with another woman who was not yet eligible for marriage. Julia was so relieved she hugged Calling Bird and then brought her to the wedding lodge to translate to Hunts In Sky. From that night forward Calling Bird helped Walks In Spring come to Hunts In Sky's sleeping lodge while Julia went to Calling Bird's lodge to sleep.

~ * ~

Jake stubbornly refused to give up the search for Julia. They had been searching for over two weeks and hadn't seen any sign of Julia or the Indian tribe. Luke wanted to go to the nearest town and find a guide, someone who might know where to look, but Jake refused to leave the area and Luke wouldn't leave him there alone. Amos continued to help the brothers, but Jake was Luke's responsibility. When Amos volunteered to go down the mountain, Luke worried about him traveling alone in the mountains. There would be no way of knowing if Amos got lost or attacked, but he insisted on going anyway.

"Jake, how long do you plan to stay up here looking for her?" Luke sat at the edge of a stream washing his feet.

Jake pulled on a boot and looked at his brother. "As long as it takes. I won't leave until I have Julia with me."

"Have you thought about what has happened to her over the past few weeks? If she's alive, she's been living with Indians all this time, and you know the stories we've both heard about what happens to white women captured by Indians. One of the braves will take her as his wife soon, if it hasn't happened already. What are you going to do if we do find the tribe? Fight all of them for her?"

Jake looked at the water and skipped a rock across. He didn't answer for a long time. "Luke, I know you don't understand this, but I *have* to find her. I don't care what has happened to her. I love her and I want her back. We should have listened to her, Luke. We should have just left Montana and went somewhere to start over. Going back to Lincoln was foolish."

"You can't look back like that Jake, it'll only hurt. We both thought it was the right thing to do. There was no way of knowing it would turn out like this, so we can't blame ourselves for something we aren't responsible for."

"No, but I can blame Ebenezer Franklin. I'm going to kill him for it," Jake said as he stood and walked to his horse. "Let's go Luke."

~ * ~

White Dove gathered berries in the warm fall sunshine. Her stomach had begun to protrude and she smiled at the thought of being a mother. She wiped the tears from her eyes and took a deep breath. Jake was gone, she knew that, but she couldn't help wishing he was there to share in this miracle they'd created. She was happy she had become pregnant, considering the way things had turned out, and more so that she wasn't with her uncle any more. She didn't know what he would've done if he'd found out she was carrying Jake's child. She was also glad that she didn't wind up married to the Englishman in San Francisco. White Dove didn't even want to think what would have happened to her in that particular situation.

The weeks slipped by and the tribe prepared for winter. They moved the village to a lower elevation, a beautiful valley with a river running through it surrounded by tall mountains. Calling Bird explained the tribe always wintered in the valley where the snows didn't fall as deep. Piles of furs had been made into clothing, moccasins, robes, and bed coverings to protect the people from the winter cold. They had dried meats and fish, and meal made from acorns and dried corn to make bread, and squash. Julia was surprised at how efficient the Indian people were and how misinformed she'd been about them.

Having heard they were savages who killed whites for no reason, Julia had been afraid of all Indian people, but now White Dove knew the Indians were more civilized than her own people. The Indian people had no need for a legal system because there was almost no crime among them. Disagreements were settled peaceably, and anybody unable to settle their dispute took them to Runs Like Wind and his decision was accepted as final. The people helped one another and no one was left to fend for themselves. It was a true community based on the idea that each person was dependent upon the other for survival, and it reminded Julia of the stories she'd read about King Arthur of Camelot.

The first snowfall reminded White Dove of Christmas and she felt a pang of longing. Until she felt the baby move and smiled. Her belly had grown round and large. Runs Like Wind had found out she'd been trading sleeping space with Walks In Spring, and so given Walks In Spring to Hunts In Sky for his wife as well. Now Walks In Spring was also expecting a baby and Julia was happy for the couple. Julia didn't consider herself Hunts In Sky's wife, they'd never had intimate relations, but he was still responsible for the care and protection of both women. It was a good arrangement for them all.

~ * ~

"We're glad you're back Amos. Do you have any news for us?" Jake said as he and Luke helped unload the items Amos brought from town. There was more ammunition, flour, sugar, coffee and cornmeal, and Amos also laid down a wanted poster with Jake and Luke's likeness on them. There was a five hundred dollar reward on each of their heads. They looked at each other and Amos grinned.

"Five hundred a piece? Looks like we're famous outlaws." Luke elbowed his brother.

Jake shrugged. "I could live without it."

"I did find out where the tribe has their winter village, or at least where it's supposed to be. I think it's reliable enough," Amos said and glanced from Luke to Jake.

"Then let's get going," Jake said, already heading off to saddle Horse.

"Hold up a minute, little brother," Luke told him. "We have to have a plan. We can't just go marching in there. They could shoot us off our horses."

"Here." Amos tossed each of the men a package as a distraction. "Merry Christmas!"

Jake and Luke looked at each other with surprise, then at Amos. They opened the packages and found warm coats inside. "Is it Christmas? I didn't realize we'd been up here so long," Luke said.

"It's not Christmas yet, another week or so I think," Amos replied. "But you need somethin' warm. It's gonna get a lot colder up here before it gets warmer."

"Thanks, Amos," Jake said as he slapped the man on the back. "Now where are we going?"

~ * ~

Julia thought she waddled like a duck. Her belly was so large she couldn't see her feet, and she had difficulty getting up and down to her fur-covered pallet. Calling Bird had become her best friend, even though the girl was only fifteen years old. They continued to share a hut, now there wasn't even the pretense that Julia slept with Hunts In Sky. Still considered his wife, it afforded her protection in the event another tribe raided the village. Now that it was full winter, no one worried about being raided, only about keeping the fires going and the children fed and warm.

White Dove was restless and didn't feel like herself. Her back ached, her feet were swollen, and she wanted to take a walk. Wearing their warmest skins and furs she and Calling Bird walked a trail through the snow that led to the river. Julia had learned to fish with the crude nets the tribe used, as well as using long sticks with the ends whittled to a point. She had the fishing stick with her today since her stomach was so large she couldn't bend over to use the nets. She wasn't sure she wanted to fish either, but she just couldn't find anything to alleviate the restlessness she felt, or the ache that had settled in her back.

~ * ~

Jake, Luke, and Amos reached the river and left their horses hidden in the forest. Having spotted the village earlier, they decided the only way to get into the village would be to leave Amos in hiding with the weapons while Jake and Luke walked in unarmed. Outnumbered, they knew it would be foolish to go in firing weapons, especially since they had no desire to hurt anyone. Jake just wanted Julia back.

Just as the brothers were about to step from the cover of trees, Luke held up one hand and pointed. Jake followed Luke's direction and saw two Indian squaws walking toward the river's edge. One was very large with the baby she was expecting and the other one looked very young. This was more than Jake and Luke had hoped for. If they could take the two squaws hostage, they'd have some bargaining power with the tribe. They waited until the two women stopped by the water, and then very carefully and quietly, came up behind the two females. Luke and Jake each put one hand around them to hold them and the other hand over the women's mouths.

Though the two men were careful not to hurt their captives, who didn't even try to fight, the pregnant one covered her stomach with both hands as if to protect her baby, and the younger one just closed her eyes and waited. Jake and Luke took them into the forest to where Amos waited with his gun in hand. The women were carefully released and Amos motioned with his pistol for them to sit on a fallen log.

When they sat down, White Dove looked the men over and then began to smile. Her eyes filled with tears and she opened her mouth but the words clotted in her throat. She was so overcome with emotion she couldn't speak for a moment.

With a deep breath she finally said, "Jake?" She spoke quietly, and he just stared. He was heavily bearded, but Julia recognized him. "Jake," she said again. He took a step toward her and she stood.

"Julia?" He said in disbelief.

Julia guessed she could understand his incredulity, her hair was greased and braided, her face was rounder, and her stomach was enormous.

"You, you..." He didn't seem to know what to say. *That's a first. Jake speechless!*

"Luke," Julia turned to him. "You're both alive. How? I don't understand."
Jake stood in front of her with his mouth gaping open.

Luke answered. "It's a long story, Julia. We've been looking for you for a fair while now." He went to her and put his arms around her. "I'm glad you're all right. They've treated you well?"

"Oh, yes. They have been very good to me." She turned to Calling Bird and introduced her. "This is Calling Bird, she's been my best friend through all of this, and she took care of me after the stagecoach rolled. I was hurt, my head I think, I don't know. I was sick for a long time after. She's also taught me her language."

Julia explained to Calling Bird in her own language who the men were and that she didn't need to be frightened because the men wouldn't hurt her. Then she turned to Amos. "Hello, Amos. I see you got tangled up in this mess as well." Julia smiled gently, thankful for whatever help he'd been able to give Jake and Luke.

"Miss Julia," Amos said politely. "I s'pose I did, but it was my choice. I overheard what your uncle was plannin' and I just couldn't let you get sent to England."

"Thank you, Amos." Julia smiled gratefully and kissed his cheek. The man blushed and nearly tripped over his own feet.

"Little brother, are you all right?" Luke slapped Jake on the shoulder. He still hadn't moved.

"I, well, I'm not sure. Julia, I can't believe we've finally found you," he said, staring at her stomach. "I-I don't know what to say."

Julia grinned, she knew he thought she'd been with one of the Indian braves and carried another man's child. "You could put your arms around me and tell me you've missed me and love me."

"I have, uh, I do, but-but..."

"But what?"

114

"But I wasn't expecting this, for you to be, well..."

"You weren't expecting me to be with child?"

He nodded, stepped toward her and put his arms around her very carefully. His mouth found hers and he kissed her.

Julia welcomed him, reveling in the feel of his mouth on hers, his tongue mating with hers, and she breathed into his mouth. "Oh, Jake I've missed you. I thought you were dead. I thought they'd hanged you." She ran her hands all over him, trying to convince herself he was really there. She still couldn't believe he was actually alive.

"I know, I know. I'm sorry, Julia. I'm so sorry." He paused. "I know you did what you had to do to survive and I don't blame you. But I don't know what to do now. I love you so much and I wanted to find you, to take you with me, and now that I see, well, you can't travel like that. I don't know what to do." He continued to hold her and ran his hands up and down her back.

"You love me?"

"More than my own life," he said, exhaling heavily as he obviously attempted to control the strong emotions inside him.

Pulling away from him, she looked into his eyes. "I love you, too, Jake. And you're right, I can't travel because your child is going to be born in just a few weeks."

She saw the flicker in his eyes and felt him stiffen as what she said registered in his mind. He grasped her shoulders and his fingers dug into her.

"Are you—you... *what?*"

"Jake, let go of my arm, you're hurting me," she said softly.

115

"Oh." He looked at his hands and released her. "I'm sorry, I just... did you... I'm..."

"Jake, you're going to be a father," Julia said and stroked his face.

"The baby is mine?"

"Of course he's yours!" she said indignantly.

Luke began to laugh. "Well, little brother, what do you say about that?"

Jake stared at Julia. "Are you sure?"

Julia's smile faded and her hands fisted at her side. A fire lit her green eyes and there was a dangerous edge to her voice. "What do you mean *am I sure*? You listen to me Jacob Isaiah Dobbs! I've been living up here in the mountains with these people, who have been very kind to me, thinking you were dead and the only thing that has gotten me through this is the fact I had your baby growing inside of me. I've been up here seven months and I am eight months pregnant, so figure it out for yourself!"

She poked a finger in his chest. "And don't you dare look at me like that and ask me if I'm sure. You're the only man I've ever been with and if you don't believe me, then get back on your stupid horse and leave me be!"

A grin began to curve Jake's lips as he wrapped his hand around the finger Julia still pressed into his chest. "Julia, I'm sorry. I love you, darlin', with all my heart. I love you." His voice was hardly more than a whisper.

"Good. Now you'll have to take me back to the village because my husband will want to meet you."

"Whoa! Wait just a minute! What do you mean your *husband*?"

116

Rie McGaha

It was Julia's turn to grin smugly, but she did explain to the poor man. "Because I'm pregnant the tribal leader, Runs Like Wind, gave me to Hunts In Sky so I'd have someone to protect me, but he's really in love with Walks In Spring, so she's married to him as well. I live with Calling Bird, so keep your shirt on. But this is their village and you'll have to speak with Runs Like Wind and Hunts In Sky. I don't know what they will say about all this."

Jake's head was spinning by the time Julia finished her explanation. Since he was obviously dazed, Julia turned to Calling Bird. "What do you think will happen?"

Calling Bird shook her head. "I have never heard of this happening before."

They decided that Jake and Luke would go into camp with the women and leave their weapons with Amos. They wanted to appear as non-threatening as possible.

As they walked into the village everyone stopped where they were and stared at the heavily bearded men. Julia smiled and spoke in the Indian language and told everyone there was nothing to fear, the men weren't dangerous. When they reached Runs Like Wind's lodge, he invited Julia inside. After she explained what had happened, he immediately stood and went outside. Julia followed him and introduced Jake and Luke. Runs Like Wind told Calling Bird to summon Hunts In Sky. When Calling Bird returned with the other man, Runs Like Wind explained the situation and then left Hunts In Sky to decide if he wanted to release Julia from their marriage.

Hunts In Sky looked at Julia, and she silently pleaded with her eyes for him to release her. A tall man with broad shoulders, he was muscular from the hard work he did. He was also a grateful man and knew Julia could have prevented him from being with the woman he loved, but instead, she had helped by bringing Walks In Spring to him while she slept with Calling Bird each night to allow them privacy. He would not prevent her from being with the man she loved, the man who had given her the child so near to being born.

Hunts In Sky stepped in front of Jake and stood with his arms crossed over his big chest. Jake met his gaze, and didn't flinch or look away. After a long moment, Hunts In Sky spoke.

Julia translated for him. "He is happy with his wife, Walks In Spring, and is proud he has created a child with her. He said because of me, he is able to be with the woman he loves and he knows I will be a good wife to you." With tears in her eyes she hugged Hunts In Sky and thanked him for his generosity.

Jake held out his hand and Hunts In Sky looked at it, not understanding the gesture. Julia explained to him it was the white man's way, so Hunts In Sky took the proffered hand.

Runs Like Wind nodded his approval and told them Julia was no longer Hunts In Sky's wife. Then he took Jake by the arm and grasped Julia's hand. Locking their hands together, he made the announcement that Jake and Julia were now husband and wife, and the pair was escorted to the wedding lodge. Julia instructed Calling Bird to make sure Luke and Amos were fed and warm and given a place to sleep as she was led away.

Inside the wedding lodge a fire was burning and a fur-covered bed waited.

Rie McGaha

Jake looked at Julia and smiled. He was nervous and didn't know why, but he took her hand and they sat together on the furs. She looked like a squaw and he smiled as he thought of what a proper lady she'd been when he had kidnapped her all those months ago. That girl was gone, and in her place was a beautiful woman who could obviously endure even the most difficult of situations. He was so very proud of her.

"I don't know what to do," he confessed quietly. "I'm afraid I'll hurt the baby if I touch you."

"I think it will be fine if you touch me. I know Hunts in Sky and Walks in Spring are still in love and she is almost as pregnant as I am. My stomach is so big I don't know how we'll manage but I want to feel your hands on me. I've missed you so much, Jake."

He stroked her cheek and kissed her softly. She removed her moccasins and leggings and then Jake helped her get out of the deerskin dress that had been modified to fit her growing stomach. Julia lay back on the furs and watched as Jake undressed, and then he lay pressed against her side.

"How do you feel?"

"Wonderful," she sighed. "I don't know how I've managed all this time without you."

"You'll never have to be without me again. I promise," he said against her mouth.

"What are we going to do, Jake?"

"We're not going to worry about anything right now, darlin'. We'll stay here if the chief will let us, and all you're going to think about is having a healthy baby. There's nothing more important to me in this world as you and our baby."

~ Ten ~

Jake, Luke, and Amos received the education of a lifetime.

Like most whites who'd come west, they'd heard about the savage Indians who attacked settlers for no good reason. But after living with the Indians for a short while they came to understand more about what the whites had done to the Indians. Besides taking valuable land and moving the Indians by force, they'd also killed the buffalo and other game the Indians depended upon for survival. They'd brought disease such as influenza and small pox to the tribes as well. It was as much a contrast from what the men had heard as the term savage was to how the tribe actually lived. Compared to the tribe, the white men were the savages.

The people in the Indian village lived peacefully with one another and the little conflicts or disagreements that did arise were settled without bloodshed. The people thrived on a real sense of community in a way the men rarely saw white people do. Sure, in times of trouble, the whites would help one another in a limited sort of way, but for the Indians, this was a way of life. The men hunted together and game was shared equally no matter who had killed the most. The women cared for all the children equally whether they were biologically related or not, and they shared equally in the daily chores of cooking, preparing hides, and making clothing. The women also planted the gardens, gathered the wood, kept the fires going, and fished the rivers and streams.

Rie McGaha

Since winter was upon them, there weren't as many chores as during the spring and summer, but there was entertainment. Men and women visited one another, told stories, and participated in snowball fights with the children. Jake got the idea to make the children sleds from stiff deer hides and wood he carved with his knife. They were crude, no doubt, but the children had fun. He also showed them how to build snow forts and snowmen, and he came to think he just might make a pretty good father after all.

By the end of January, Julia was sure the baby would come any day. She had grown so large she could barely move, her legs and feet were constantly swollen, her back ached all of the time, and she swore she'd never peed so much in her life.

Jake rubbed her back and massaged her feet at night. He didn't tell her so, but he thought she had never been as beautiful as she was with her belly full and round like it was now. He also didn't tell her that she'd also never been as grouchy as she was lately! And for her sake, he hoped the baby would hurry and come quickly so she didn't suffer an overlong bout of labor. The women had told her there were herbs they would brew into a tea for her when the time came that would make the labor go more easily. Jake hoped they were right because he didn't want to see her in pain.

Julia woke in the middle of the night. The ache in her back seemed to be getting worse, and no matter how she turned, she couldn't get comfortable. She tried to not wake Jake, but as soon as she moved away from him, he woke.

"Are you all right?"

"I don't know." She paced back and forth with her hands pressed against her lower back. "My back won't stop hurting. It's been aching all day and now it seems to be getting worse."

"Do you want me to get Laughing Woman?" Jake was more than a little afraid of Laughing Woman. She was very old, with a way of looking at a person that made them think she could see inside of them. He couldn't figure out why she was called Laughing Woman either, because he'd never heard her laugh even once. He thought maybe it was like one of the ranch hands he and Luke had worked with. The man's name was Tiny and he was anything but.

"No. Yes. I don't know. Let's just wait a little while and see. I'd hate to wake anyone up for no good reason. I have all this extra weight so my back is bound to hurt, I guess." She groaned, paced a few more steps, then walked back to their bed.

"Here," Jake said as he gently took her arm. "Sit down and I'll rub your back. Maybe it'll help you go back to sleep."

She sat down heavily and he began to massage her back. It did help some and she leaned back against him gratefully. Jake nipped her shoulder and she smiled, but then a pain wrapped around her stomach and her eyes went wide in surprise.

"Jake, I think you should get Laughing Woman now," she gasped.

"Now?"

"Yes." She clutched her abdomen. "Right now!"

Jake pulled on his britches, then slipped on his moccasins and dashed outside into the freezing cold before he realized he hadn't even bothered with a shirt. He didn't care as he ran to Laughing Woman's lodge and called loudly to her. He would have thought at her age he'd have to call her several times before she answered, but she appeared almost immediately. He took her by the hand and hurriedly led her through the snow to the hut he and Julia shared.

Julia's face was twisted in agony as another contraction gripped her and Jake dropped to his knees beside her. Laughing Woman spoke softly as she moved her bony hands over Julia's bare stomach. Laughing Woman sent Jake to wake Calling Bird and Little Flower, while she prepared an herbal tea for Julia to drink.

When Jake returned with the other two women, Laughing Woman tried to send Jake outside, but he refused. He didn't speak much of the tribe's language, but he understood more, and had no trouble making the woman understand he wasn't going anywhere. Laughing Woman peered intently at him for a long moment and then nodded.

Jake sat at Julia's head with crossed legs and her head resting against his thigh. He rubbed her shoulders and spoke soothingly to her, but he was as nervous as she was and he just couldn't imagine doing what she was about to do.

Luke went to the lodge periodically and called to Jake just to make sure his brother was doing all right. Things seemed to be going well and Luke offered his prayers for the mother and child's good health.

Julia labored for the rest of the night and well into the morning. The entire tribe waited with Luke and Amos, but the atmosphere was party-like. To the tribe, the birth of a child was cause to celebrate. Like everything else, a good hunt, a bountiful crop, they were all considered good reasons to celebrate.

Amos had spending a lot of time with Babbles Like Brook, a young squaw who seemed to have eyes for the little man almost from the first moment he'd come into camp. Luke wouldn't be at all surprised if Amos asked Runs Like Wind for the maiden's hand by spring. As for himself, Luke just didn't see himself settling down to a wife and kids anytime soon—if ever. Not that he didn't think it was a wonderful thing, he'd just never been of a mind to spend the rest of his life with only one woman. There were just too many of them in all shapes and sizes for him to be expected to pick one.

Just before noon, Julia screamed with one long, hard contraction and the baby's head appeared. Julia had such a grip on Jake's hand that he thought she'd surely break a few bones, but when he saw the little head appear, he forgot about his hand. Julia took another breath and pushed with all her might and Jake watched the shoulders and chest appear, and then the slippery baby boy slid right into Laughing Woman's hands.

She laid the baby on Julia's chest, tied off the cord with a piece of thin leather, and Jake used his knife to sever it. The baby squalled as Julia held him gently and cried in happy relief against his dark head. Jake held them both and cried with her. He'd never witnessed anything quite like that in his life and was speechless with emotion.

Rie McGaha

"You have a son, Jake," Julia said with awe as she kissed him.

"No, *we* have a son, Julia. And I've never seen a better looking boy in my life."

Julia laughed and kissed him again. "What are we going to name him?"

"I don't know," he said as he rubbed the little cheek with his finger. "What was your father's name?"

"Nicholas," she said softly.

"My father's name was William. How about we name him after both of them?"

"Nicholas William Dobbs," Julia said aloud. "Unless you'd rather have your father's name first?"

"No, I think Nicholas William is a fine name," he said softly and watched his son nuzzle at Julia's breast. "Well, at least he knows what to do there," Jake said and smiled as his son suckled greedily.

Julia looked up at Jake and smiled. "Now we will have to take him to Runs Like Wind for his Indian name."

"Runs Like Wind will name him?"

"That's what Calling Bird told me. Is that all right with you?"

"Yes." He nodded and kissed her forehead. "If it wasn't for him and the people here, I don't know what would have become of you. By attacking the stage, they prevented you from being married to the Englishman and taken to England. I don't even want to think about what would have happened to you or our son then. He saved your life and our son's life. I'll always be grateful to him."

The women cleaned the lodge and took away the bloodied hides. The afterbirth was saved and

Laughing Woman handed it to Jake. Jake took it and looked blankly at the old woman and then at Julia.

Julia smiled as she explained. "She says you have to bury it so that in the spring it will nurture the ground. Life begets life."

"Fine," he said and raised a brow. "And I'll do that right now. I'll also tell Luke that he's got a nephew." He kissed Julia and his son before leaving the lodge with his hands full.

Little Flower took the baby from Julia, carefully laid him down and began to wash the blood from his body and hair. Then he was dried and wrapped in a warm fur and given back to Julia. The other women left her warm and comfortable, sleeping with her newborn son asleep in her arms.

When Jake entered the lodge he stopped and caught his breath in amazement at the sight he beheld. He'd never thought to see his own wife and child sleeping this way. A year ago he'd been wondering if he'd even survive the winter, let alone be alive right now to see his wife and son. Feelings of protectiveness and possessiveness welled up within him and overwhelmed him.

He fell to his knees and, though he'd not prayed much in his life, he closed his eyes now and simply said, "Thank you."

He crawled to the pallet where his family was and lay down behind his wife. Leaning up on his elbow, he watched the two of them. *Julia is so beautiful*, he thought, and she'd worked so hard to give his son life, he was amazed at her strength. He traced his finger gently over his son's cheek and thought of how much the baby's face was shaped like his mother's. He could see the same bone structure, the same nose and chin, but the baby's hair was dark like his and Jake wondered if the boy would have Julia's green eyes or blue ones like his own. It didn't matter, not really. Jake Dobbs had a son, and his beloved back, and he was a very happy man.

He leaned over and kissed Julia softly on the cheek. She stirred and opened her eyes. She smiled up at him. "How are you?"

"I'm great," he said and smiled. "How are you doing?"

"I'm tired, but I feel all right."

"I was just looking at him. He's so perfect. And he looks so much like you."

Julia looked at the baby. "You really think he looks like me?"

Jake nodded. "I do."

"But he's got your hair color and he's big too," she said. "He definitely gets that from you."

"Thank you, Julia," Jake whispered hoarsely.

Julia smiled. "Thank you, Jake. I've never been happier in my life."

He rested his head on his arm, holding his wife close with his fingers resting on his son's arm. He closed his eyes and the three of them slept peacefully, with the fire burning low and the snow falling quietly outside.

~ Eleven ~

Summer was coming. Jake could feel it and smell it in the air. Sitting outside, he looked around, he was content here with the tribe, his wife and son, but he knew he had something to take care of and he needed to talk to Julia about it. He'd been up for nearly half the night talking to Luke and Amos. It was time to go back to Lincoln and clear their names.

Amos had married Babbles Like Brook and didn't want to leave the village he now called home. He didn't care what happened back in Lincoln, he was no longer a part of it. Jake and Luke understood his feelings and decided to make the trip back without him.

Jake looked at his wife weeding the garden with the baby wrapped snugly in the wood framed papoose on her back. She dressed like the other women and except for her green eyes and lighter hair, it was difficult to tell she wasn't an Indian squaw. He smiled at her when she looked up from her work. He would wait until later in the afternoon and then ask Calling Bird to mind the baby while he took his wife for a walk along the river. He wasn't looking forward to the conversation but he'd put it off as long as he could.

Runs Like Wind had given Jake and Julia's son his Indian name when the baby was eight weeks old. He'd also given Jake an Indian name, indicating he was a member of the tribe as well. Baby Nicholas was called *Eyes of Eagle* because the boy seemed to never miss a thing. From the time he was old enough to begin staying awake for any period of time his eyes constantly darted back and forth as if he was afraid of missing something. Jake was now called *White Feather* because of the way his hair had grown long with a single white streak. Julia thought the name was fitting and often teased him that watching her give birth had caused the streak to appear.

Jake and Julia walked hand-in-hand along the river bank. They strolled along comfortably without saying anything as they listened to the wildlife and the liquid sounds of the river. Eventually, they sat on a rock and kicked off their moccasins to dangle their feet in the cool water.

Julia waited, knowing Jake would tell her what he'd brought her out here for in his own time. She suspected it had to do with her uncle, and she was prepared.

"Luke and I have been talking about going back to Lincoln," he said simply.

She held his hand and stared at the water as it rushed by. "You know I'm going to tell you I don't want you to go."

"I know, but it's something we've got to do or we'll never be able to show our faces again. You don't have to go if you don't want to, but it would help if you did. There's no telling what your uncle has done since trying to send you to San Francisco. He might have told them I've killed you. You're the only one who can prove to everyone we're innocent of kidnapping and murder."

Julia looked out at the water for a long time before she looked at him. "I'll go, but not to Lincoln. We can go to Helena and talk to the sheriff there. I don't trust anyone in Lincoln, least of all my uncle. If you and Luke will agree to that, then I'll go."

"I think that's a good idea. I don't know why it didn't occur to me first," he said with a grin, then pulled her closer and kissed her cheek. "What about Nicholas? I don't know if it's safe to take him with us, but I know you won't want to leave him here either."

She knew he was right, it might not be safe for Nicholas in Helena but there was no way she would leave her baby. It might be months before they could return to the tribe, if they even came back at all. She thought about leaving the people who'd been her family for well over a year now, and she didn't want to. She hadn't realized until now, but she was happy here and the village was her home. She didn't really care about living among white people again, and she couldn't care less about silk dresses, fancy balls, money, or any of the extravagant things she had once thought were so important. Julia looked at Jake and thought of the baby they'd made together, and she knew there was nothing as important as what they had now.

"Will you make me a promise, Jake?"

"If I can, you know I will." He'd vowed to never make promises he'd not be able to keep, and she knew he was a man of his word.

"When it's done, we'll come back here."

"You want to come back here? I thought once everything was settled you'd want to live in Boston and see our son raised like a real gentleman?"

She smiled. "If you'd asked me that a year ago, you'd have been right. But now I don't want any of that. This is our home. This is where I want to raise our son, and where I want to live with you for the rest of my life. I can't imagine being anywhere else now."

"Life isn't easy here, Julia. Maybe after we've been in Helena for a while you'll change your mind and want to stay in town. I want you to be happy, darlin'."

"Do you want to live in town, Jake?"

He looked across the river and inhaled deeply, then exhaled sharply and said, "No, I don't, but Luke does. He's lonely here and I think once everything is settled he'll want to stay. I don't know how it'll be if he stays and we come back here. I'm his only family, well, you and Nicky, too, but I don't want him to be all alone."

"He's a big boy, Jake. He'll always know where we are, and we can go for visits, too, if he does decide to stay. Who knows, he might decide after a while that it's not all he thought it would be and come back."

"I love you, Jake," she said and smiled against his lips.

"I love you, Julia. I always will," he said and kissed her again, then carried her into the water.

Julia hadn't worn one of her dresses in over a year and felt strangely uncomfortable in the gingham material now. She felt awkward as she tried walking in the stiff leather boots with their metal hooks and high tops. Hopefully, the trip would be quick so she could go back to wearing the soft, supple deerskin dress, leggings and moccasins she had gotten used to.

After saying good-bye and shedding tears with Calling Bird, Laughing Woman, and the others, Julia stood before Runs Like Wind with tears in her eyes. He stared at her with his arms crossed over his broad chest and said nothing. After a moment Julia hugged him and found he actually hugged her back, but when she pulled away, he crossed his arms over his chest again and said nothing.

Jake helped her onto his horse and handed Nicky up to her, then mounted Horse behind them. Jake and Luke looked back as they rode into the forest and Amos held his hand up in one last good-bye. They waved briefly and then entered the woods.

All three of them were silent as they started the long, hard trip back to Helena. Julia sniffled now and then, but it was the only evidence she had yet to stop crying. She held Nicky close to her and wondered if the trip would be as ill-fated as she felt it would be.

~ * ~

Helena was hot, dry, and dusty this late in the year. It was also a rapidly growing city and crowded with both people and livestock. New businesses were built as more and more people came from the east, and there were now two hotels to choose from. Jake and Luke rented rooms and made sure Julia and Nicky were settled in with a hot bath and some good food. Jake went to the mercantile and purchased diaper cloths, pins, and blankets for the baby, then went back to the hotel and took a bath. It had been a long trip and tomorrow would be soon enough to pay a visit to the local sheriff.

The next morning, the three of them ate breakfast together, then Jake walked Julia and Nicky back upstairs. "Don't leave this room for any reason and don't let anyone inside, no matter what." He kissed her deeply and locked the door, then he took a deep breath and looked at Luke. Luke grinned and shrugged, and they walked together down the street to the sheriff's office.

And spent most of the morning telling their story, retelling it, and answering the lawman's questions.

The law in Helena was a big-bellied man with white hair who appeared to be in his fifties, yet he was really only forty-five. His name was John Joseph Walker and he'd been a lawman for twenty-five years. First back east in Boston, then he'd moved west to St. Louis, and farther west again until he was in Helena, Montana. He'd been U.S. Marshall here for the past ten years. Big John was the law in the western district of Montana, and though most of the towns had their own sheriffs, Big John was the one who kept an eye on all of them.

He had to travel to Missoula from time to time, but he didn't mind since the federal judge there, Tom Walker, was his little brother. Big John was an honest man and he didn't put up with anyone who wanted to use his town for criminal activity. He'd run into a few hooligans who'd come to town with the idea of taking over, but it didn't take long for all of them to decide Montana wasn't the place for them. He didn't put up with cattle rustling, horse stealing, bank robbin', or anyone who thought to mistreat a woman, child, or animal.

He'd married Martha Kay Williams right around the same time he'd gotten his first job as a deputy and they'd raised four daughters and two sons over the years. Martha went back to St. Louis and Boston every couple of years to visit those children, and the eighteen grandchildren they'd all

133

managed to produce. Big John went along on one or two of those trips, but mostly he could wait until they all came to visit him in Montana.

Big John still looked at Martha the way he had all those years ago at a church picnic one sunny Sunday afternoon when he'd still been *Johnny* to everyone who knew him. Martha still liked to tell the story of how tongue-tied John had been around her, and she told it with a gleam in her eye. Big John and Martha remained very much in love.

Between being a lawman and a father of six, John figured he could read a person just about as well as anyone, and guessed the only one who'd know the intents and purposes of another person's words better than he did would be God Himself. And, as he sat at his desk, leaning back casually in his chair, with the air in the office growing warmer with the day, he listened to these two brothers tell their story.

He'd heard it all before, at least he'd heard the other side of the story that made these two out as kidnapping, murdering, thieves. Now they said the girl they supposedly kidnapped and murdered was very much alive and with them willingly, and it had been her uncle who had sent her off to California to marry a stranger in exchange for money. It had also been her uncle who had stolen her inheritance to pay his own debts, and her uncle who had shot one of these boys sitting in front of him.

Big John tapped his pipe, set it on the tray on his desk and leaned forward. With his elbows on the desk, he steepled his fingers together and looked steadily at both of the men before him for long moments without saying a word. Big John was not one to jump to conclusions about anyone, but he'd met the girl's uncle personally and he hadn't liked him one bit. That hadn't meant he didn't believe the story the uncle told, it just meant he'd wanted a little more proof of the truth before he issued warrants and started running around the country with a posse looking for these two boys. He could see the two in front him were nervous but he was used to making men nervous, especially those as young as these two. He figured they'd be about the same age as his own boys, and Big John had been making Mike and Cody nervous for years now.

He looked at the brothers over his fingers and cleared his throat. "Where's the girl now?"

Jake and Luke looked at each other. "She's at the hotel," Jake answered.

"It would sure help if I could see for myself that she's all right and not being held against her will. You think she'd be willing to do that?"

"Yes sir," Jake nodded. "But..." Jake looked at Luke and cleared his throat again.

"But what, Son?" Big Jake sat back in his chair again.

"She's afraid of her uncle doing something to me and Luke. And now that we've... " Jake hesitated again. He didn't want to tell the Marshall they'd had a baby without getting married first, and he didn't want the Marshall to think he didn't want to do the right thing, or that Julia was a loose woman. He looked up at the Marshall, then said with a steady voice, "We have a baby and Julia's afraid her uncle will do something to her and the baby when he finds out."

"I can see where that'd be cause for her to worry," Big John said with a nod. "Why don't the three of us walk on over to the hotel to talk with Miss Cavanaugh and see what she has to say?"

They climbed the hotel stairs together, Big John bringing up the rear. Jake tapped on the door and called out, "Julia, it's me," before he put the key in the lock and turned the handle. He poked his head in first and looked around. Julia was rocking Nicky on her lap and smiled at him. He pushed the door open and the three men walked into the room.

"Julia, this is Marshall Walker. He wanted to meet you." Jake introduced the man.

"Miss Cavanaugh? Pleased to meet you." Big John held his hat in his hand and crossed the room to stand near Julia so he could take a look at Nicky. "That's a handsome boy you've got there."

"Thank you, Marshall. And it's nice to meet you as well," Julia said as she smiled up at the man.

"I need to ask you a few questions," Big John said and took the chair he was offered. "Jake and Luke here have told me quite a story and I'd be interested in hearing what you have to say."

"I don't really know where to start," Julia began and passed the baby to Jake. "Would you like some tea, Marshall? Luke could go down and get some."

"Thank you, but not right now." Big John smiled affectionately at the girl, she was pretty and bright and he could tell she had been well-educated and was very intelligent. "Why don't you just start at the beginning and tell me whatever comes to mind first?"

"My parents were killed a few years ago and my uncle was designated to look after me until I married, or reached my majority. I came to Montana by train and lived with my uncle until I met Jake."

"I'm sorry about your parents, but where did you live before your parents died?"

"Boston. I was born there and lived my whole life there until their death."

Big John looked thoughtful for a moment. "Was your father Nicholas Cavanaugh by any chance?"

Julia's smile brightened. "Why yes! Did you know him?"

"Nicholas and Elizabeth Cavanaugh?"

"Yes." Julia's dimples showed in both cheeks. "Are you from Boston, Marshall?"

Big John chuckled as he looked at her. "Your father and I had more than one occasion to meet, him being a lawyer and all. That man infuriated me in the courts. I left Boston a long time ago and went to St. Louis before coming here. I'm sorry to hear he's passed on, he was a good man."

"Thank you, Marshall." Julia smiled, though a little sadness shone in her eyes. "I met Jake when he kidnapped me out of my uncle's yard..."

Big John looked at Jake and Luke, and Jake grinned a lopsided grin. "You said you didn't kidnap her." Big John raised a brow.

"Well..." Jake started.

"It was love at first sight," Julia said, coming to stand next to Jake, and placed a protective hand on his shoulder. "Or at least it was love at first sight as soon as he let me off his horse and untied me so I could look at him." But she smiled and Big John could see she told the truth.

Over the next two hours Julia told the entire story to the Marshall, including how she was sold to a man in California who was supposed to marry her and take her to England with him. She told him about the Indian attack and how her uncle's men were killed, about the Indians who took her captive, and she told of the months she spent with the tribe while her belly grew round with the baby Jake didn't know they'd made.

When she finished, Jake added, "The only reason we haven't gotten married is because there hasn't been the chance. The chief married us, but I know it won't be recognized here in town. I'd like to marry Julia just as quick as we can get all of this settled."

"I want the three of you to write down everything you just told me and sign it. Then bring it over to the office in the morning. And as far as I'm concerned, once that's done, you're all free to go. I'll make sure your uncle knows all about it personally, and there won't be any problems from this for you in the future. If there is, you just get word to me and I'll take care of it."

Julia wrapped her arms around the big man and kissed his cheek. "Thank you, Marshall. Thank you so much!"

Luke shook the Marshall's hand. "I don't know what to say, but thank you."

"Yes, thank you, Marshall," Jake said and shook the big man's hand with both of his.

"First thing you can do is go on over to the church and marry this young lady properly," Big John said with a grin.

"Yes, sir," Jake said and shook his hand again. "I'll get right on that."

~ Twelve ~

"You may kiss your bride," Reverend Purcevell said, smiling at Jake.

"Yes sir." Jake grinned wide and looked at Julia. He held her face in both hands and kissed her lips gently.

"Congratulations," the preacher said and shook Jake's hand.

"Thank you, Reverend."

"Yes, thank you," Julia said and pecked the preacher's cheek.

"Come here," Luke said as he settled Nicky to one side so he could kiss his sister-in-law. Julia grinned and took the baby from him.

"Let's go over to the hotel and have a wedding dinner," Jake said, throwing one arm around his brother's shoulders as the other went around his wife.

They walked out of the little church, leaving the preacher standing at the altar, grinning as he watched them go.

Neither brother ever thought to feel such relief in their lives. It was all behind them, the worry over going to prison, being hanged, or getting shot by Ebenezer Franklin and his men. It was finally over, they had Big John's word on it, and right now, all they wanted to do was have a good supper to celebrate. In the morning they'd discuss what they would do for all the days of their future. They walked together down the wooden sidewalk toward the hotel, waited on a wagon to pass by, and then stepped into the street.

Jake didn't remember anything in particular, it all seemed to happen in slow motion. Julia's scream rang in his ears. Nicky's startled cry. The sound of gunfire. The sight of Luke falling to the ground, while his blood ran onto the dirt.

Jake grabbed Julia and Nicky in both arms, pulling them to the ground, as he rolled on top of them. When he came to his feet, he had a .45 in each hand. With only a split second to see where the shot came from, he fired his weapons. Unloading both guns, the sound roared in his ears, as smoke filled the air, clogging Jake's throat and burning his eyes. Then just as suddenly, all was quiet. Jake lowered his arms and looked around.

He walked slowly through the smoke toward the man he shot, and when the smoke cleared he could see three men lay dead in the street and Big John stood grinning at him. Jake suddenly remembered Luke and quickly shoved the guns into their holsters, then turned and ran back to his brother. Julia was leaning over Luke, his head in one hand, while she tried to comfort Nicky with the other.

"Is he alive?" Jake dropped to his knees and covered the wound in Luke's chest with his hands. "Get a doctor," he shouted to no one in particular. "Luke! Luke! Luke, wake up!"

"I'm awake! How could anybody possibly sleep with you screaming at the top of your lungs?"

"You're alive. Thank God, you're alive."

"Here now, boy." Big John's big hand settled on Jake's shoulder. "I've got some men here that'll take him over to the doc's place. Come on Jake, tend your wife and son, we'll take care of your brother."

Rie McGaha

"Julia, are you all right?" Jake turned to her and Nicky and saw tears running down her cheeks.

"I'm okay," she said and nodded. "I was so scared I didn't know what to do."

"It was your uncle's men. Come on, let's get over to the docs and see how bad Luke is."

They waited while Doc Thompson worked on Luke and removed the bullet from his shoulder. "How do you feel, Luke?" Jake leaned over him.

"I'd feel a whole better if people would quit shooting me."

"Your brother is a lucky man. Another inch or so to the left and he wouldn't be breathing right now. It looks like this wasn't his first time to catch a slug either," the doctor said with a shake of his head.

"No, it's not. Is he going to be all right?" Jake went to the washstand and rinsed Luke's blood from his hands.

"I can't answer for myself?" Luke said, and then coughed.

The doc went to him, and checked his wounds again. "He'll be just fine. I want him to stay here overnight just to make sure he don't get the fever, but I'm betting he'll be on his feet in a day or two."

Jake looked at Julia and let out a sigh of relief. "Thank you, Doc."

Big John came out of the room where he'd been talking to Luke. "He didn't even see it coming. He's darn lucky though, I could just as easy be seeing him over to the undertaker right now." Big John looked at Jake. "You know who you killed?"

Jake looked at Julia, then back at the Marshall and shook his head.

Big John grinned. "You killed the one with his head in the horse trough. That was Haney Logan, a hired gun out of Chicago, Son. I'd heard Ebenezer Franklin hired him, but I didn't know he was even in town till you killed him."

"Are you going to arrest me?" Jake asked as he looked at Julia and his son, who'd settled into his mother's arms and gone back to sleep.

"Arrest you?" Big John threw back his head and laughed. "Naw, Son, I ain't arresting you. I am going to give you the reward though."

"Reward?" Jake and Julia said together.

"Yep. There's ten thousand dollars on that man's head. Dead or alive."

Jake's mouth fell open and he heard Julia gasp. "What are you talking about? Ten thou— how is that possible, Marshall?"

"He's been wanted for years now. He's a hired killer and he's assassinated some top government officials over there in England, France, and down Mexico way too. Lawmen all over the world have been trying to bag ol' Haney Logan." Big John laughed again. "They'll won't believe it when they find out a youngster like you did the job they couldn't."

"Who else got killed out there?"

Big John looked at Jake, then at Julia. "I'm sorry, ma'am, but your uncle was one of 'em. I killed him myself, so don't be thinking your husband here had anything to do with it."

"My uncle's dead?"

"Yes, ma'am. I'm very sorry about that. I had no choice though. He would've killed Jake if I hadn't shot him first. The other man was one of Franklin's men, and there was one more that I didn't recog-

Rie McGaha

nize, but I imagine he was a hired gun as well. They were planning on killing all of you I think. Even you, ma'am. Otherwise they wouldn't have fired with you standing so close."

"That..." Jake said through gritted teeth, but held his tongue. He was mad again at the thought his wife and son could just as easily be laying where Luke was now, or worse.

"It's over now, Son. Don't worry about it anymore. In a few days, you'll have your reward and you can do whatever you want to with it. I imagine you'll need to go to Lincoln and settle your uncle's affairs, ma'am. His ranch and other holdings all belong to you now, Mrs. Dobbs."

"I don't know," Julia said hesitantly. "I can't think about any of this now. We just got married."

"Take your time. Nothing has to be settled tonight. You two take that baby on over to the hotel and find something to eat. Get some rest and come back in the morning to see about Luke. I'll leave a deputy here just in case. If he needs you, the deputy will fetch you. Now go."

~ * ~

"It's yours now, Luke," Julia said as she handed the deed to him.

"What do you mean it's mine? This is yours, Julia. Franklin owed you this and more." Luke shook his head. His arm was in a sling, but he was healing just fine. Maybe he hit his head harder than he thought.

"We want you to have it, Luke." Julia smiled gently.

"Yep," Jake nodded. "We're going back to the People. We want to stay there for a while."

"But..." Luke began.

"But nothing, big brother. This is the life you wanted remember? A ranch close to town, bars, and women. You'll be just fine."

"What about you, Jake?"

"I have everything I need," Jake said, pulling Julia closer to him. "Besides, we want the baby to be born with Laughing Woman there."

Luke looked from Jake to Julia, and Julia nodded with a wide grin. "We'll have another baby by spring," she told him.

"Well, I'll be," Luke said softly. "When will you leave?"

"In a few weeks. We want to make sure your shoulder's completely healed first," Jake said.

Rie McGaha

~ Epilogue ~

They named the baby boy Morgan Jacob, and his twin sister, Katherine Julia. Luke didn't know what to think as he looked at the two of them. They were so small, wrapped in soft blankets in their mother's arms. Luke wondered what his brother and sister-in-law would think when they learned he had twins named after both of them. He chuckled to himself. What would they think when they found out he married Ruby Red?

He guessed they wouldn't be any more surprised than he had been to discover he was in love with the girl. Having gone to the saloon a few times, he gambled a bit after Jake and Julia went back to the Indian village. He was lonely, he could admit to that, and living on the ranch was a dream come true, but it was hard work. Hard and lonely work without his brother.

On one visit into town, Ruby Red sat in his lap, and no matter that the girl was a whore, she sure was a pretty one. He went upstairs with her. After that, he spent every Friday night with her. In the beginning he told himself it was just a physical thing. After all, she'd not done anything to him she hadn't done with at least a hundred other men. He knew he couldn't be all that special to her, but somewhere along the way, she'd become special to him.

~ * ~

Ruby was her real name, Ruby Jane Morgan, and she was from Kansas City. They'd spent a lot of time together, and sometimes they just laid on the bed talking all night long. Luke had never done that with a woman before. She told him how her father had died before she was even born, and her mother had taken in laundry and scrubbed floors to feed herself, but just barely did anyway. After Ruby was born, her mother did all she could to take care of the infant but she just wasn't able to, and left her at the foundling home hoping the nuns there would take care of her, raise her, and teach her to read and write.

They raised her all right. They taught her to read and write, and when she was twelve the man that came looking to adopt, picked Ruby out of all the girls there. The only question the nuns had was whether or not he had the cash required to reimburse them for the cost of raising her.

He was the first to call her Ruby Red, what with all her red hair cascading down her back, and he dressed her in fine dresses made from silk, satin, and lace. He took her to his fine, big house and showed her to her bedroom. That was when she met Mama Ruth.

Mama Ruth ran the house, she ran the girls, and anyone who didn't obey found out real fast how ruthless Mama Ruth could be. Ruby Red was a beautiful red-haired, blue-eyed virgin and when the bidding on her finally ended, the man paid one thousand dollars to have her for the night. Ruby Red found out that night it was a lot easier to let the men have their way than to fight them.

Even after ten years in the profession, Ruby Red was still beautiful, still vibrant, and part of her was still very young and sweet. That side of her was what Luke had fallen in love with. When he realized he was in love with her he didn't go into town for nearly a month. How could he love Ruby Red? How could he expect to make her his wife and not be ridiculed? For four weeks straight he fought with himself.

Then one night he rode into town, went straight to the saloon and looked around until he spotted Ruby Red just coming downstairs, getting ready to start work for the evening. She smiled broadly when she saw him, but he only gritted his teeth, walked up to her, pulled her up against him and kissed her like it was the first time either of them had ever been kissed.

Then he told her he loved her. He told her she was going to marry him. And then, with her mouth hanging open, he picked her up and carried her out of the saloon. He yelled over his shoulder to the barkeep that Ruby Red had just quit her job. He tossed her on his horse and swung up behind her.

That was over a year ago, and now she lay in his bed holding his daughter and son, her face glowing in spite of the hours she'd just spent bringing them into this world. And Luke couldn't have been happier.

It hadn't taken long for Ruby Red to become Miss Ruby when she went into town. And the few men who looked Ruby up and down and made lewd comments loudly enough for everyone, including Luke, to hear, found themselves face first in the dirt. It didn't take long for everyone to figure out Luke loved Ruby no matter what she may have been. It was what she was *now* that was important. She was Ruby Dobbs, wife of Luke Dobbs, and now the mother of the most beautiful babies Luke had ever laid eyes on. And he couldn't wait until Jake and Julia found out.

He didn't have long to wait.

~ * ~

Rie McGaha

The twins were nearly three months old and summer coming to an end. Luke was out mending fences with the men and Ruby was gathering eggs in the henhouse. Ruby liked living on the ranch, the hens, and gathering eggs. She liked working in the dirt growing vegetables, flowers, and making a home and a life with Luke. She had never dared to dream before of such a life, but now that it was hers, she knew every step she'd taken in the past had been one closer to where she was now. She would have changed her past, if given the chance, but not if it would change where she was now. Whatever it took to be here, to be Luke's wife and the mother of his children, was all worth it. She was a happy woman.

Ruby walked out of the henhouse with a basket full of eggs just as horses came through the gate and into the barnyard. She shielded her eyes and stared, trying to figure out who had come calling. It took her a minute, and then she recognized them both. Jake and Julia Dobbs. Ruby felt her heart leap and she hoped they would accept her. She wanted them to so badly.

"Hello," Jake called out. "We're looking for Luke. I'm his bro... Ruby Red? What are you doing here?"

Luke rode in late that afternoon and unsaddled his mount before turning the animal loose in the corral. He noticed the strange horses and wondered idly who had come for a visit. Stopping at the well, he pumped some water and washed the dirt from his hands and face before going inside. When he walked into the kitchen he stopped dead in his tracks. There at the table was Ruby with Jake and

Julia, and all three of them were laughing and talking like old friends.

"Jake? Julia?"

"Luke!" Jake jumped to his feet and wrapped
his arms around his brother. Julia hugged him too.
Luke was so overcome with emotion he couldn't
even speak.

Jake and Julia had come home with Nicky,
who was now nearly three years old, and his younger
brother, John Lucas Dobbs, was already toddling
about the house. John wasn't able to run exactly,
and spent most of his time falling down, but he
chased Nicky everywhere. Julia's stomach had begun
to swell with the newest addition to the Dobbs' family, who would be arriving in just over five months.

Jake and Julia decided to stay with Luke and
Ruby while their house was built on the east side of
the property near the creek. It had been Julia's fa-
vorite place when she'd lived there with her uncle.
The copse of trees, along with the babbling brook
and its grassy banks made a peaceful place, and that
was where she wanted their house built. She had no
desire to live in the house her uncle had once owned, even though Luke and Ruby said they'd happily
give it to them. It was Luke's house. His, Ruby's, and
their children's, and Julia was just happy a real family lived there now. That it was Luke's family was
even better.

When the house was finally finished the fol-
lowing summer, Big John and his wife came down
from Helena and stayed a few days with them. They
had become like grandparents to the youngest
Dobbs', and Big John's wife had never been happier.
Martha always said that if she couldn't have her own

Rie McGaha

grandchildren nearby, she was content to spoil her adopted ones whenever she could.

They sat around the rough-hewn wooden table beneath the shade of a tree eating fried chicken, corn on the cob, potato salad, baked beans, and apple pie. Babies were held, little boys played in the dirt, and conversation and laughter filled the air. Jake looked around the table at each face and felt a lump form in his throat.

This was what he'd wanted his whole life, to have a wife and children, to see his brother content and in love. Good friends, good food, and the best family in the world. Jake Dobbs was a happy man. He swallowed hard, leaned over and kissed Julia on the cheek. She looked up at him and smiled. A cry from behind them brought Jake to his feet. Nicky had tripped over a stick and skinned his knee. It was a wound only a dad knew how to tend.

~ End ~

www.ingramcontent.com/pod-product-compliance
Lightning Source LLC
Chambersburg PA
CBHW070934130626
46555CB00001B/434